Someone tapped Trish on the shoulder. "Is there room for one more?"

She turned in the pew. Jack stood in the aisle. And little Tommy answered, "Sure!" before she could say no.

When Jack sat down, Trish found herself wedged between him and her son. She hadn't been this close to Jack since that long-ago prom night....

Trish's insides turned weak and trembly. This was too intimate. Sitting beside him in church. Sharing a hymnal. Their son—the son Jack didn't know he had—at her side.

Her heart clenched. This was the life she'd wished for, prayed for, dreamed of all those years ago. Once, she'd worshiped the ground Jack Krieger walked on.

But she'd learned her lesson after that long-ago night.

She glanced at the man beside her.

No matter how charming, no matter how attractive, no matter how tempted, she couldn't—wouldn't— let her heart be hurt that way again....

Dear Reader,

Calling all royal watchers! This month, Silhouette Romance's Carolyn Zane kicks off our exciting new series, ROYALLY WED: THE MISSING HEIR, with the gem *Of Royal Blood*. Fans of last year's ROYALLY WED series will love this thrilling four-book adventure, filled with twists and turns—and of course, plenty of love and romance. Blue bloods and commoners alike will also enjoy Laurey Bright's newest addition to her VIRGIN BRIDES thematic series, *The Heiress Bride*, about a woman who agrees to marry to protect the empire that is rightfully hers.

This month is also filled with earth-shattering secrets! First, award-winning author Sharon De Vita serves up a whopper in her latest SADDLE FALLS title, *Anything for Her Family*. Natalie McMahon is much more than the twin boys' nanny— she's their mother! And in Karen Rose Smith's *A Husband in Her Eyes*, the heroine has her eyesight restored, only to have haunting visions of a man and child. Can she bring love and happiness back into their lives?

Everyone likes surprises, right? Well, in Susan Meier's *Married Right Away*, the heroine certainly gives her boss the shock of his life—she's having his baby! And Love Inspired author Cynthia Rutledge makes her Silhouette Romance debut with her modern-day Cinderella story, *Trish's Not-So-Little Secret*, about "Fatty Patty" who comes back to her hometown a beautiful swan—and a single mom with a jaw-dropping secret!

We hope this month that you feel like a princess and enjoy the royal treats we have for you from Silhouette Romance.

Happy reading!

Mary-Theresa Hussey

Mary-Theresa Hussey
Senior Editor

Please address questions and book requests to:
Silhouette Reader Service
U.S.: 3010 Walden Ave., P.O. Box 1325, Buffalo, NY 14269
Canadian: P.O. Box 609, Fort Erie, Ont. L2A 5X3

Trish's Not-So-Little Secret

CYNTHIA RUTLEDGE

SILHOUETTE *Romance*®

Published by Silhouette Books

America's Publisher of Contemporary Romance

To my editor, Patience Smith. I can't begin to tell you
how much your constant support and encouragement has
meant to me. And even though "our" title isn't on the
cover, I'll never be able to think of this book without
thinking of that title, and of you.

 SILHOUETTE BOOKS

ISBN 0-373-19581-8

TRISH'S NOT-SO-LITTLE SECRET

Visit Silhouette at www.eHarlequin.com

Printed in U.S.A.

CYNTHIA RUTLEDGE

is a lifelong Nebraska resident. She graduated from the University of Nebraska with a liberal arts degree, then returned several years later to earn a degree in nursing. A registered nurse, Cynthia now works full-time for a large insurance company and writes in the evenings and on weekends. She loves writing romance because a happy ending is guaranteed! She is the author of five books for Steeple Hill's Love Inspired series; this is her first book for Silhouette Romance.

Cynthia loves to hear from readers, and encourages you to visit her Web site at http://www.cynthiarutledge.com.

Trish's List of Things to Do:

☐ Enroll little Tommy in swimming lessons

☐ Send out résumé

☐ Ignore Jack Krieger

☐ Buy a swanky dress on the off chance Jack will
   see you in it (although he doesn't deserve to
   after the way he treated you in high school)

☐ Tell Tommy that playing basketball with
   that nice Jack person is not a good idea
   (even though he is Tommy's father)

☐ Buy new curtains for the living room

☐ Stop peeking out the window at Jack playing
   basketball with disobedient son

☐ Get a loaf of bread and milk

☐ Continue to ignore Jack Krieger

Chapter One

"Patty Bradley? Is that you?"

Trish's fingers clenched the stem of the crystal goblet. It had been ten years since she'd heard that voice, but she recognized it immediately.

Ignoring a momentary impulse to run, Trish took a leisurely sip of wine and turned. "Why, Jack Krieger, what a surprise."

Five years in public relations had served Trish well. Strong and steady, her voice gave no indication of the sudden tightness that gripped her chest at the sight of him.

"I hardly recognized you." Jack took a step back and stared, his gaze openly admiring. "You look wonderful."

"You don't look so bad yourself," Trish said, keeping her tone light and offhand.

All these years she'd told herself that he wasn't really as attractive as she'd remembered. But she was wrong.

The toffee-colored hair of his youth had deepened to a warm chestnut and his vivid blue eyes, once the color of the sky on a clear summer day, now glowed like dark sapphires. Age had only added depth and maturity to the boyish features she remembered so well. If Jack had been handsome at eighteen, he was devastating at twenty-eight.

Life had obviously been good to him. His smile was genuine and he wore the easy self-assurance of someone who knows his place in the world.

She should hate him. His lies and deceit had taken the last of her innocence. But it wasn't easy for Trish to hate anyone, much less Jack Krieger. Still, she was no fool. She'd never forget how he'd used her.

Trish hardened her gaze.

Jack took a sip of his wine and smiled, apparently not noticing.

"I can't believe how you've changed," he said with a flash of perfect white teeth. "You look terrific."

"Thanks." Trish accepted the compliment graciously. Even she, who'd never been all that confident about her appearance, had to admit that tonight Jack was right. She looked fabulous. She'd taken extra time with her makeup and dressed with special care, trying to bolster a flagging confidence that had been seriously shaken by the recent un-expected loss of her job.

But she knew his admiring look had less to do with her makeup and clothes and more to do with the svelte figure beneath the silk sheath. In his mind he was seeing the girl she'd been in high school, the girl that had been good enough to sleep with in secret but not good enough to be his girlfriend in public. His dowdy next-door neighbor, the one kids loved to tease. He was remembering Fatty Patty.

Fatty Patty.

Trish forced a deep breath and released it. How the horrid name still hurt. Even years and distance and success hadn't been able to completely erase the memories of her classmates' cruel taunts.

But that was ten years ago, and she'd come a long way since those days. Trish Bradley had proven she was a survivor.

"I never thought I'd see you again," Jack said finally. "After graduation it was like you'd dropped off the face of the earth."

"I hardly think Washington is off the face of the earth," she said lightly.

"It might as well be." He shot her a penetrating stare. "No one knew where you were. You never even wrote."

Trish smiled and forced a shoulder up in a care-less shrug as if cutting all ties with Lynnwood had been of no consequence. In truth, it had been the first of many difficult decisions she'd had to make.

"Honey, aren't you going to introduce me?" Pete Minchow, Trish's escort for the evening, took the momentary silence as an invitation to join in.

"Pete, I don't think—"

"I don't believe we've met." Without missing a beat, Jack extended his hand to the other man. "I'm Jack Krieger, an old friend of Patty's from high school."

It was all Trish could do not to groan out loud. There he went again, pulling in the past along with that ridiculous name. But somehow it didn't sound so ridiculous when he said it. Actually it never had.

"Pete Minchow." Pete shook Jack's hand as if he was priming a pump. Originally from Texas, the man had the good-ol'-boy image down to a science and used it to his advantage in his business dealings. But Trish knew that beneath that country boy exterior beat the heart of a shrewd businessman. "Pleased to meet you. Any friend of Trish here is a friend of mine."

"Trish?" Jack's brows drew together in a frown. "What happened to Patty?"

Pete gazed at Trish for a moment. "Patty, eh? I kinda like it."

"Well, I don't." Trish plucked a piece of lint from the collar of Pete's tux. "And if you ever call me that, you're a dead man."

She smiled and took a sip of her wine.

Pete's eyes widened for a second, then he chuckled with good-natured humor. "I'll have to remember that."

"Do you work for the government, Pete?" Jack tilted his head questioningly as if he was really interested in what Pete had to say. It was the same look he used to give her when they'd sit on her porch swing and she'd tell him about her day.

Her heart twisted at the memory.

"Pete owns his own business." Trish looked up at the lean, tall Texan suddenly grateful to have such a handsome man at her side. "He's not into politics. Or playing games."

Jack cocked his head and studied Trish for a moment before turning his attention back to Pete. "I thought everybody in this town had something to do with politics."

"Lord, no," Pete said with a laugh. "I'm into cars. New, used, buy, sell, lease, you name it, and I've got 'em. We're one of the largest GM dealers on the eastern seaboard."

"Really?" Jack said. "Impressive."

Although the words sounded sincere, Trish had to wonder. They were, after all, living and working in a town where you ate, slept and breathed politics. Few would find owning a car dealership impressive.

"So, have you and Patty been dating long?" Jack asked.

"Don't you mean *Trish?*" Pete gave Trish a

wink and took a sip of wine. "What's it been dar-lin'? Five? Six months?"

"Something like that," she said, grateful Pete was keeping his mouth shut about the nature of their relationship. They were merely friends with an understanding. She accompanied him to an occasional party if he needed an escort and he did the same for her.

It was the need to network that had caused Trish to forgo popcorn and a movie with Tommy and accept Pete's invitation to one of the hottest parties in D.C. The event was the perfect opportunity to make contacts and get some leads on a new position.

It had been two months since she'd been restructured out of her dream job with one of the top PR firms in Washington. Corporate downsizing they'd called it. All she knew was that once her savings ran out, the wolves would be at the door. Anxiety nipped at her, but Trish had been through worse times and survived. Even if just one of her prayers were answered, she'd be okay.

"She took back her maiden name after they split. That's been what? Six or seven years?" Pete turned toward Trish with an expectant look.

"A long time," Trish said.

Pete had obviously been repeating the same lies she'd been telling everyone for years: that she'd married out of high school and divorced shortly after. It was a little fabrication that easily explained the presence of a now-nine-year-old son and no husband.

"You're divorced?" Jack blurted out, his eyes wide with surprise. "Your grandmother never even told me you'd married."

"Then I bet she never told you Trish has a son, either?" Pete said.

It was all Trish could do not to give him a swift jab in the ribs. Would Pete ever learn to keep his mouth shut?

"From my," Trish raised her chin with a cool stare in Jack's direction, "first marriage."

"First marriage?" The muscle in Jack's jaw jumped. "You've been married more than once?"

She'd never been married, never planned to marry. But that was her business, certainly not his.

"Sometimes life just doesn't work out the way we want." Trish lowered her voice, being purposefully mysterious. But the words hit too close to home, and her tone turned sharp. "Not that it's any of your business."

"Now, darlin'. I know you're just having some fun, but the man thinks you're serious." Pete put his arm around her and gave her a big squeeze. "Jack, I've known Trish for quite a few years and, as far as I know, she's only been married once."

"So you have a little boy," Jack mused.

"Tommy's a cute kid," Pete said, when Trish didn't respond. "But he's not all that little anymore."

"How old is your son?" Jack's gaze shifted to Trish.

Trish thought quickly. Had she mentioned to Pete that Tommy had recently turned nine? And even if she had, would he remember?

"He's eight." She lifted the glass of merlot to her lips and took a sip.

"That old?" His brows drew together. She could almost see the wheels turning in his head. "But then you must have gotten pregnant—"

"About a year after I left Lynnwood. That next spring." Trish said, chopping a whole year off Tommy's age. Thankfully, Jack would never see the boy. Tall for his age, Tommy could more easily pass for ten than eight.

"Were you living in D.C. then?"

The question was probably completely innocent, considering they hadn't seen each other for so long, but the more she talked the more likely she was to trip herself up.

"That was so long ago." Trish waved one hand carelessly.

"Do you ever miss Lynnwood?" Jack's gaze never left her face.

"Not really." She drained the last of her wine from the glass. "There's nothing for me there."

"There's friends and fam—" Jack stopped suddenly. She knew he was remembering that her grandmother had been her only relative and that she'd died earlier in the year. "Well, what about friends? Don't you miss them?"

"Oh, puh-leeze." Trish rolled her eyes. "We both know I was hardly Miss Popular. Actually I don't think I had any friends back then."

"Yes, you did," Jack said.

She quirked an eyebrow questioningly.

"You had me," Jack said softly. "I was your friend."

Trish lifted her chin and met his gaze, willing him to see in her eyes what she couldn't, wouldn't say in Pete's presence. That a friend never would have done what he did to her.

"Where in the heck is this Lindwood place anyway?" Pete munched thoughtfully on a tiny wafer topped with salmon, seemingly oblivious to the electricity crackling in the air.

"Actually it's Lynnwood," Jack said, slanting a glance at Trish. "It's a small town in Kansas, about twenty miles northwest of Kansas City. Patty, uh, I mean Trish, and I grew up there."

"I love those little bumps in the road." Pete washed down the salmon with the last of his wine. "Sometimes I think about moving back to Texas, to my hometown. But then I remember that I've got more cars on my lot than there are people in that godforsaken place and the urge passes."

He laughed and grabbed another drink from a passing waiter. "So tell me Jack, do you still live in Lindwood?"

This time Jack didn't bother to correct him.

"Lynnwood is still home," Jack said, glancing at Trish. "But right now I'm living in Arlington."

A chill traveled up Trish's spine. She and Tommy lived in Vienna, only a few metro stops away.

"Great. You have a business card on you?" Pete smiled. "I'll give you a call and maybe we can all get together sometime."

"I'd like that." Jack reached into his pocket. He pulled out a silver holder, extracted a card and scribbled some numbers on it before handing it to Pete. "Lunch usually works for me."

"Wonderful." Pete grabbed the card and shoved it into his pocket. "Tell me, have you ever been to that little Greek place over by Dupont Circle?"

Jack paused for a moment, then shook his head.

"Let me tell you it may look like a dump, but their food is the best. You'll love it."

"I'm sure I will," Jack said. His gaze shifted to Trish.

She forced a smile. As far as she was concerned, Pete could circular file Jack's business card the second he got home.

Because there was one thing she knew for sure...it would be a cold day in hell before she'd willingly have anything to do with Jack Krieger again.

Chapter Two

"Well, here it is." Trish waved her arm in a sweeping gesture. Littered with boxes and suitcases, the parlor bore little resemblance to the neat-as-a-pin room her grandmother had reserved for company. But the light filtering through the picture window lent a cheery air and, although dated, the flowered wallpaper was free from stains. "What do you think?"

She turned to her son and crossed her fingers. Moving back to Kansas had been a decision born of necessity. Her lease was up, her savings account at zero and her only Washington job prospect wasn't hiring until September. It only made sense to return to Lynnwood where she and Tommy had a place to live that wouldn't cost her a dime.

When she'd inherited the house after her grandmother's death, she'd planned to sell it, but something had held her back. Though the years she'd spent in Lynnwood hadn't all been happy, this house had been the only home she'd ever known. Now, with her world crumbling around her, it beckoned to her like a lighthouse promising shelter from stormy seas.

And, at least in Lynnwood she didn't have to worry about running into Jack. Their chance meeting in D.C. two months earlier had made her decision to move back easier. It was funny when you thought about it, he was now in Washington and she was back in Lynnwood.

"This place stinks." Tommy dropped a box overflowing with pots and pans to the floor.

Her heart sank. Everyone had told her that Tommy might resent moving, but up to now he'd been fairly upbeat.

Trish took a deep breath and forced a reassuring tone. "I know it's hard to move to a new place. But it will get easier. I promise."

"It's not hard," Tommy's gaze widened in surprise. "I like it here."

Trish's brows drew together in confusion. "You said it stinks."

"It does." Tommy took a deep breath and wrinkled his nose. "Yuck. Take a big whiff."

Trish followed his example and inhaled deeply. She promptly sneezed.

"What'd I tell you?" He nudged a basketball on the floor with his shoe, then bent to pick it up.

"It's not that bad." Trish laughed and tousled his hair. "The place is just musty from being shut up so long. Once we get some air in here it should be fine."

Tommy's look was clearly skeptical.

"C'mon. Help your mom out and open some windows."

He glanced longingly out the front door, the basketball now spinning between his fingers. "I thought maybe I could shoot some baskets before dinner."

"I'm afraid that hoop you're staring at belongs to our neighbors," Trish said remembering how Mr. Krieger had put up the hoop at the beginning of Jack's freshman year.

"They won't care if I use it."

Trish hesitated. Moving next door to Jack's mother had been Trish's main reservation about returning to Lynnwood. But she'd convinced herself that she and Tommy would be so busy they wouldn't have time for any over-the-fence socializing.

"Honey, we just moved in. I don't even know the neighbors." It was a tiny lie but there was no way Trish was going to ask a Krieger for anything.

"Can't I just ask?" Tommy grabbed her hand, a pleading look in his eyes. "Please?"

Her heart twisted at the disappointment on his face but she shook her head. "How 'bout if we go to the park as soon as we get everything out of the van? That will be more fun, anyway. There'll probably be some boys there who you could play with. If not, I might be persuaded to shoot a few hoops."

"Thanks, Mom." His arms flew around her and he hugged her tight. "You're the greatest."

She hugged him back, stroking the back of his hair, enjoying the moment of closeness. Tommy was no longer her little baby. He was a growing boy who was turning out to be the spitting image of his handsome father.

Trish had spent many sleepless nights worrying that Mrs. Krieger would take one look at Tommy and make the connection. But she'd eventually decided she was being ridiculous. As far as the Krieger family and everyone else was concerned, she and Jack had barely known each other.

Tommy started to squirm, and Trish dropped a kiss on the top of his head before letting him go. "Why don't you grab your suitcases from the car and take them up to your room?"

He hesitated, and she met his gaze with a motherly firmness that had become second nature after nine years. "The sooner the van is unpacked, the sooner we go to the park."

Tommy headed out the front door and Trish reluctantly bent over to pick up the box of kitchenware Tommy had left behind.

"Knock, knock." Connie Krieger's head peered in through the back doorway. "Anybody home?"

Trish straightened abruptly and wiped her sweaty palms against her jeans. "Come in."

She recognized Jack's mother immediately. Although the woman must be in her midfifties, she still looked as young and stylish as Trish remembered. Her dark hair held no hint of gray, and only laugh lines edged her hazel eyes. Dressed in khaki shorts and a red polo, she could almost pass as Jack's sister.

"Patty?" The woman hesitated. Her gaze dropped to take in Trish's long slender legs in formfitting blue jeans before rising to the tiny T that clung to Trish's curves like a second skin. "I don't know if you remember me. I'm Connie Krieger. I live next door."

"Of course I remember you, Mrs. Krieger." Trish politely took the hand the woman extended and shook it firmly.

"Please call me Connie."

"Only if you call me Trish," she said smoothly. Trish found it hard not to return the woman's smile, but the last thing she wanted was to become "neighborly" with Jack's mother.

The front screen closed with a bang. Trish and

Connie both turned in time to see Tommy streak past the doorway and head up the stairs.

Connie raised a questioning brow.

"My son, Tommy," Trish explained. "He's nine."

Tommy's age flowed from her lips automatically, and although Trish would have given anything to call her words back, it was too late. If she said anything now it would only draw more attention to the gaffe.

"My grandson, Matt, will be nine next month. It's been so long since my son was small that I'd forgotten how busy they are at that age." Connie chuckled and shook her head. "Ninety miles an hour, twenty-four seven."

"I know what you mean." Trish laughed, and in spite of her reservations, found herself warming to the woman. "Tommy told me he wants to play football *and* basketball *and* baseball. I tried to explain most kids just choose one. But he said how could he pick? He likes them all."

"I know just what you're going through," Connie said with an understanding smile. "My son Jack was like that, too. Fortunately in a small town, kids can pretty much do it all."

Footsteps sounded again in the hall and a second later, Tommy burst into the room. "Mom, I cleaned out the van and opened the—"

Tommy stopped short. "I'm sorry."

Trish smiled reassuringly. "Tommy, this is Mrs. Krieger, our neighbor."

Trish shifted her gaze to Connie. "Mrs. Krieger, this is my son, Tommy."

Tommy stepped forward and extended his hand. "It's nice to meet you, Mrs. Krieger."

Her heart swelled with pride. From the time he was little, she'd stressed good manners. It looked like some of the teaching had paid off.

"Nice to meet you too, Tommy." Connie smiled warmly and took his small hand in hers. "I live right next door so if you ever need anything, you just come on over."

Tommy's eyes widened. "You live in the house with the basketball hoop?"

"That's right." Connie's dimples flashed and she glanced at Trish. "I understand from your mother that you like to play."

Tommy nodded. He lowered his gaze for a second and took a deep breath. "Would you mind if I came over sometime and shot some baskets? I'd be real careful. I promise not to hit your car."

Trish stared in horror. "Honey, Mrs. Krieger was just being n—"

"Of course you can come over," Connie said. "That is, if it's okay with your mother."

Trish's breath caught. Her gaze slid from her son's hopeful face to his grandmother's curious one. It would be so easy to say yes.

But Trish had learned long ago that the easy way
was not always the right way. Allowing Tommy to
play over at Connie Krieger's house would be sheer
madness. Nothing good would come out of such
closeness except trouble.

And she'd had enough of that to last a lifetime.

Jack eased the rental car into his mother's driveway and pulled to a stop, breathing a sigh of relief.
The plane ride from D.C. to Kansas City had been
bumpy and he'd run into a thunderstorm on his way
back to Lynnwood.

He got out of the car and stretched. It was good
to be home. And to see the sun shining.

Jack shifted his gaze, expecting his mother to
come racing out to greet him. When the front door
remained closed, he glanced around, noticing for
the first time that the Buick was gone.

Suddenly it hit him. His mother golfed every
Wednesday afternoon. It'd be hours before she'd
be home. Opting for an earlier flight out of National
had seemed like a good idea, but now he was left
at loose ends.

He could go see his sister. But with three children under ten, Julie's house would be buzzing.
And right now, relaxing with a cool brew sounded
infinitely more appealing than wrestling with his
nephews.

Unpacking the car only took a few minutes. After setting the bags inside the foyer, Jack grabbed a beer from the refrigerator and headed back outside.

The rain that had dogged his drive home had passed through the small town earlier in the day, leaving beads of water dripping from the blue spruce and the air smelling like spring.

Jack wiped the moisture off the weathered wood of the porch swing with the back of his hand and took a seat. His gaze scanned the block, taking in the well-kept two-story homes, the manicured lawns and the abundance of spring flowers. He'd grown up on this block. Some of his best memories had been in this neighborhood, on this porch. Or next door, on Patty's steps.

His gaze shifted to his left, to the house barely visible through the trees. A sudden movement and a flash of red caught his eyes. He set the beer on the floor and moved to the railing. Jack narrowed his gaze.

Someone must have finally moved into Granny's house.

Patty's grandmother had been ''Granny'' to all the neighborhood children. When she'd died shortly after Jack had left for Washington, not only had Patty lost a grandmother but the whole neighborhood had as well.

Jack stared for a moment longer, but between the bushes and the trees, he couldn't get a good look.

Impulsively he raked back his hair with one hand and headed over to meet the new neighbor, slipping through the same space in the hedge he'd used as a shortcut years ago.

Right away he saw that the neighbor was female; an attractive woman with tiny red shorts that barely covered her shapely bottom. Jack's appreciative gaze lowered to linger on the long slender legs, before moving upward to the golden brown skin covered by a bikini top. She stood on a rickety stepladder, scraping the paint from around the windows with a putty knife.

"Need any help?"

Startled, the woman whirled, the sudden movement upsetting the ladder's balance. It tilted and she gave a small cry of alarm.

Jack raced across the yard and reached her just before she hit the ground.

The final burst of energy caused Jack to stumble. But he shielded her body with his, taking the brunt of the fall. Jack remained still for a second, catching his breath and waiting for his heart to return to normal.

But the soft curves pressed against him made that an impossible task. The woman shifted in his arms, her face turning to meet his.

Jack's heart stopped.

Familiar green eyes widened.

For a second he was eighteen again, locked in a

storage closet, the air crackling with more electricity than a Kansas thunderstorm. Almost of its own volition his hand rose to lightly push back a strand of blond hair that had fallen loose from her ponytail.

Patty gasped and jerked back, tumbling from his arms to the ground beside him. She quickly scrambled to her feet, her chest heaving.

Jack raised himself up on one elbow, his emotions a tangled mass of confusing thoughts and feelings.

"Are you okay?" It was an inane remark, but the best he could do under the circumstances.

"What are you doing here?" she said, her eyes flashing.

"I might ask you the same question."

"I live here." She lifted her chin in a challenging tilt. "I moved back two weeks ago."

He couldn't hide his surprise. "You didn't say anything at the party about moving back to Lynnwood."

"I didn't make the decision until last month," she said.

The coolness of Patty's tone surprised Jack. Though she'd been standoffish at the party, he'd attributed that to her being there with a date. But she wasn't with a date now.

Jack pushed himself up to a sitting position before rising to his feet. His white shirt was grass stained, and a few twigs and leaves clung to his sleeves. He brushed them off with the palm of his hand and shot her his best smile. "Well, welcome back."

"Thank you," she said, her tone clipped. "You still haven't told me what you're doing here."

"I just got back into town." He gestured toward his house. "I'm just killing some time until my mother gets home."

Some of the tenseness seemed to leave her shoulders. "So you're only here for a visit?"

Jack's smile widened. "Actually I'm moving back, too. What a coincidence. You and I together again."

What a coincidence?

Trish stared in horror. Having him in the same town was a complication she'd never envisioned. Her stomach clenched.

"Will you be living with your mother?" She resisted the urge to cross her arms across her chest, his penetrating gaze strangely unsettling.

"I'm a little past that point." Jack chuckled. "Actually, I have my own house."

"In Kansas City?" Trish knew she was grasping at straws, but she could only hope this house of his was anywhere but in Lynnwood.

"Why would I buy a house in KC?" he said. "I work in Lynnwood."

Her heart sank. She didn't have money to move again. And even if she did, where would she go?

"I brought the old Armbruster place."

Trish's head jerked up.

"You bought the mansion?" The words were out of her mouth before she could stop them.

He smiled and the lines around his eyes crinkled. "You remember."

"Vaguely." She waved with a dismissive hand.

How could she forget? The old Victorian, known by community residents as "the mansion," had been the town's showplace for as long as she could remember.

When the Armbrusters had lived there, the place was always ablaze with lights and filled with laughter. There had been many nights, when the stars were particularly bright and the air especially warm, that she and Jack had strolled down the dark sidewalk to the end of the block, stopping to stare at the mansion.

Looking back, Trish wondered what it was about the place that had always been so appealing. Was it that the home always overflowed with people, while she felt so isolated and alone? Or was she drawn to the home because of its stability? The mansion had stood in the same place for a hundred years. It was a castle, a fortress and more a part of the town than she would ever be.

Once, when Jack had made her wish on a star,

she'd found herself wishing that the mansion would one day be her home. Of course, at the time, her childish dream had included him at her side.

Trish's mouth twisted. What a fool she'd been.

"Do you want to see the inside?" Jack reached into his pocket and pulled out a set of keys, dangling them between his fingers. "I'd love to show you around."

For a brief second Trish was tempted. Though she'd vowed to keep her distance from Jack, she'd always wondered if the place was as beautiful on the inside as it was on the outside.

Jack smiled enticingly, jingling the keys. "C'mon, Patty."

The name acted like a splash of cold water, bringing her to her senses. How did he do it? For one crazy moment she'd been tempted to go with him. But she needed to remember that Jack Krieger was a chameleon, a man who could change his colors in a heartbeat. A man who could whisper words of love one minute then laugh at her the next. He was a man who'd proven he couldn't be trusted.

"I'm afraid not," Trish said. Proper etiquette would dictate adding "some other time perhaps" or another phrase to smooth the refusal. Instead Trish lifted a brow. "And, Jack?"

His gaze met hers and for a second her heart twisted at the disappointment in his eyes. Trish couldn't understand how he could look so sincere but be so devious. Fortunately, she didn't have to understand. She only had to remember.

"The name is Trish. Patty is long gone."

"You may have changed your name," Jack said, "but you're still the same person."

"That's where you're wrong."

Sweet-and-innocent Patty had died when he'd betrayed her trust all those years ago.

The same person?

The same lovestruck fool?

Not anymore and never again.

Chapter Three

"I'm so glad you're home." Connie Krieger smiled at her son and poured pancake batter onto the griddle. "It seems like you've been gone forever."

"I hardly think a year could be considered forever." Jack returned her smile. She'd told him before he left that she was worried he'd like it so much in D.C. he wouldn't want to come back. But she needn't have been concerned. Though the time he'd spent working as a lobbyist for the Independent Community Bankers of America had been worthwhile, it had solidified his belief that the Midwest was where he wanted to be.

"It's good to be home," Jack said simply.

His mother flushed, and he could tell his words had pleased her.

This was the first time the two of them had had a chance to sit down and talk. By the time she'd returned from golfing it was late, and Jack's older sister, Julie, had dropped by with her husband and three kids. Most of the evening had been spent eating the feast his mother had prepared for his homecoming and wrestling with his niece and nephews.

"Speaking of home, I bet you're anxious to move into your new place."

"I can't wait." Jack leaned forward, anticipation surging through his veins. "I thought I'd start moving some of my things today."

Over one hundred years old, Jack's "new" place stood like a sentinel at the edge of town. He'd impulsively purchased the home at an estate auction shortly before he'd left town. And while he'd been gone, the contractors had restored the place to its original splendor.

"I'll be glad to help." His mother set a plate of steaming pancakes brimming with blueberries on the table and warmed their coffees before sitting down. "I'm afraid Grandma Irene has a bridge tournament that should take most of the day, so she won't be available, but Granddad should be home by noon. The members of his investment club are reading to the children at the community center this week."

Jack smiled at the thought of his grandfather surrounded by a bunch of grade-school children. Though he'd been good to Jack when he was growing up, the former head of the Great Plains Bank Group had always been more comfortable talking Wall Street with his cronies than Sesame Street with his grandchildren.

His son, Jack's father, had been the same way. Overseeing the banks had been his number-one priority, and from the time Jack had been small, he'd been groomed to follow in his father's footsteps.

When his dad was killed in a car accident at the beginning of Jack's senior year in high school, only Patty had understood the pressure he'd felt, the fear of being thrust too soon into a role he wasn't sure he even wanted.

Jack took a bite of pancake and thought about the first time he'd really noticed Patty Bradley.

They'd gone to the same school since they were thirteen. But between sports, hanging out with his friends and working at the bank, Jack had never taken the time to pay any attention to the girl next door. Until one Saturday night at the end of his junior year. He'd come home late from a party and was fumbling with the lock on his front door when he'd heard a feminine voice call his name.

He'd followed the sound and found Patty sitting on the steps of her grandmother's porch, a bag of chips in one hand and a thirty-two-ounce soft drink in the other. Her blond hair was pulled back into a ponytail and secured with a rubber band. Her ample figure was shrouded in a loose T-shirt and sweatpants.

His scrutiny had clearly made her uncomfortable, and her message had been short and sweet; his girlfriend, Missy, had stopped by and wanted him to call.

Jack had shrugged off the request. He and Missy had been fighting most of the week and he knew he'd eventually call her, but for now the intelligence in Patty's eyes and the bag of chips in her hand beckoned. Impulsively he'd asked if he could join her.

She'd stared at him for a moment, then offered him some chips.

He'd sat and taken a handful.

They'd talked until three.

Unlike most girls he knew, Patty wasn't out to impress him. She spoke her mind but she also listened. He'd quickly discovered she was good at keeping confidences, and they'd become friends... of sorts.

At school everything had remained the same. He'd liked being surrounded by his friends, while Patty had preferred to be alone. Or so he'd thought at the time. A fresh wave of guilt washed over Jack. Until he'd seen her at that party two months ago, he'd never considered that he'd been her only friend.

But now that he thought about it, she'd always been available. Always waiting for him. They'd spent almost every Friday and Saturday of his entire senior year together. Late at night after he'd taken his date home, long after his mother and her grandmother had gone to bed, they would sit and talk.

It had become a ritual: he came home; she would be on her porch.

She'd started having a can of his favorite soda waiting. He'd started telling his dates he had a midnight curfew.

After that first night, he'd never thought about whether Patty was beautiful or plain. Whether she was fat or thin. She was just Patty, his friend and confidante.

"Jack?" His mother's voice broke into his thoughts. "Did you hear what I just said?"

He lifted his gaze and stared at her blankly.

"Some things never change." She shook her head and chuckled. "I said isn't it wonderful that Granny's house is occupied again?"

"Did I tell you I saw her in Washington?"

"Who?" His mother's brows pulled together in confusion.

"Patty Bradley."

"You did?"

"I couldn't believe it." Absently Jack slathered more butter on his pancakes. "'Course as you know she goes by Trish now. And she doesn't look or act anything like the old Patty."

Abruptly he realized that's why seeing her had been so disturbing.

She was beautiful.

She was sophisticated.

But she wasn't Patty.

She wasn't the girl he remembered.

"The old Patty?" His mother's voice was indulgent. "Jack, you barely knew the girl. Why, in all the years she lived next door, I don't believe I heard you say two words to her."

Jack started to argue, to tell his mother that he and Patty had been the closest of friends. He stopped when he realized she'd never believe him.

"Actually we talked more than you realized," he said. "She was a great girl. You'd have liked her."

And Patty would have liked his mother, too. She'd told him more than once how much she missed her own mother. He'd listened and even commiserated. But had he done anything to help her?

Jack didn't need to ask the question. He already knew the answer. No longer hungry, he sat his fork down and pushed the stack of half-eaten pancakes aside.

"I'm looking forward to getting better acquainted with her," his mother said. "And with her son."

"I wouldn't hold my breath." Jack gathered up his dishes, rose and walked to the sink. "When I talked to her yesterday she barely gave me the time of day. I don't think she's interested in being neighborly."

"Oh, my dear. Don't be absurd." His mother laughed. "Just because she didn't fall all over you like most women do doesn't mean she doesn't like you. Trish is a lovely woman. And I have the distinct feeling she and I are going to be good friends."

Jack stared out the kitchen window. Maybe his mother was right. Maybe he had expected too much from Patty. Or maybe he was right and she really did have something against him. He took a deep, steadying breath, finding the thought strangely disturbing. With calculated deliberateness, he slowly filled a glass with water from the tap.

His gaze returned to the window. Though he didn't know all the neighborhood children by name, Jack knew them by sight. But the dark-haired boy working on his three-point jump shot in their drive wasn't familiar at all. "Who's the kid?"

His mother rose from the table and moved to the window, still clutching her cup of coffee. She stood on her tiptoes and peered over his shoulder.

"That's Tommy Bradley." His mother smiled. "He's been coming over every day to practice."

"That boy is Patty's son?" This time Jack couldn't hide his surprise.

Connie set her coffee mug on the counter and studied him. "Remember she goes by Trish now."

Jack looked out the window again and narrowed his gaze. A frown creased his brow. "That boy looks awfully big for eight."

"Eight?" Now it was his mother's turn to frown. "Trish said he was nine."

"He can't be nine."

"Maybe I heard wrong." She shrugged, a tiny smile hovering on her lips. "You sure seem interested in my new neighbor. It couldn't have anything to do with the fact that his mother, once an ugly duckling, is now a beautiful swan?"

"It has nothing to do with looks," he snapped. "And Patty was never ugly."

Her smile faded.

"I'm sorry," he said. "I don't know what's gotten into me." He hadn't been himself since the night he'd gone to the cocktail party.

The night he'd seen Patty.

The night old feelings and emotions had come flooding back.

"Jack?"

He shifted his gaze to find his mother staring.

"I was just teasing," she said. "I like Trish. I didn't mean to say anything bad about her."

"It's okay." Jack looped his arm around his mother's shoulders and gave her a reassuring squeeze as his gaze shifted out the window. "You know, it's been a long time since I've shot a ball through that hoop."

"Tommy would welcome the company," his mother said softly. "The boy doesn't complain, but I know he gets lonely."

Jack stared through the glass at the solitary figure. Without a second thought to the packing boxes sitting in his Jeep waiting to be filled, Jack headed out the back door. A gust of wind tore the screen door from his hand and it slammed shut behind him.

Tommy looked up and a watchful wariness filled his blue eyes. "Mrs. Kreiger said I could shoot baskets."

The boy held the basketball tight against his chest as if afraid that Jack would take it from him.

"Relax." Jack offered the boy an easy smile. "I'm not here to run you off. I'm Jack, Mrs. Krieger's son. I'm also an old friend of your mother's. I thought you might want to play a little one-on-one."

The boy's face lit up. "Sure."

After thirty minutes of watching Tommy scramble for the ball and sink some difficult shots, Jack concluded the boy definitely had talent. He had good balance and great hands, plus a natural athleticism.

"Time out." Jack dropped to sit on the back step. "Let's take a break."

"After you rest, can we play some more?" Sweat glistened on the boy's face, but his eyes sparkled. "My mom won't have lunch ready for a while yet."

"I'm afraid I need to get going." Jack shook his head regretfully.

"What about tomorrow?" the boy said eagerly.

"I don't think that'll work." Jack softened his refusal with a smile. "I'll be busy moving. Maybe you and your friends c—"

"I don't have any friends." The boy lowered his gaze, scuffing the toe of his sneakers against the concrete. "Not yet, anyway. But that's okay," he added quickly, "I'm used to playing alone."

Though the boy bore little physical resemblance to his mother, in that instant Jack could see reminders of Patty in his loneliness.

"I could be here by four." All Jack could think of was Patty. And how he'd taken what she'd offered him but not given anything in return. "Do you know my nephew, Matt Cullen? I think he's about your age."

Tommy nodded slowly. "He's in my class at swim lessons."

"I thought I'd ask him and his dad if they wanted to play, too." Though his brother-in-law, Dan, was coming over after work to help him move, Dan was a family man, and Jack knew he'd welcome a change in plans if it involved playing basketball with his son.

"I'd like that." Caution tempered the spark of excitement in Tommy's eyes. "But what if they say no?"

"If that happens," Jack met the boy's gaze, "then I guess it will be just you and me. What do you say?"

Tommy's wide grin was all the answer Jack needed.

He returned the smile and a warm sense of satisfaction flowed through him. Doing the right thing had never felt so good.

Trish smoothed the covers around her son. "Did you have a good day?"

She didn't know why she'd asked. From the moment she'd called him in for lunch she could see it in his face, in the spring in his step, in the way he asked for second helpings. For the first time since they'd moved, Trish had the distinct feeling everything was going to be okay.

"It was the best day ever," he said happily snuggling down in the pillow.

"Did you make a new friend?" She tried to sound offhand, as if she didn't care. Above all, she didn't want him to think it mattered to her.

Like it did to my grandmother.

Her grandmother had been a wonderful woman, but she'd desperately wanted her granddaughter to have friends.

"No, but..." Tommy thought for a moment.

Trish waited. She'd learned through trial and error not to rush her son. Eventually he would tell her everything, but it had to be in his own time.

"Matt Cullen might come over tomorrow afternoon."

"Matt?" A vague image of a thin blond-haired

boy in a pair of blue trunks flashed before Trish. "From swim lessons?"

"Mmm-hmm."

"He seems like a nice boy," Trish said matter-of-factly while breathing a prayer of thanks. This would be the first time since they'd moved to Lynn-wood three weeks ago that Tommy would have a friend over. "Are you excited?"

"I guess."

"I went to school with a Cullen. Of course he was three or four years older." Trish paused. "I wonder if that could be his dad?"

"I don't know." Tommy shrugged.

"It doesn't matter. I'll make some cookies for you and—" she stopped, suddenly remembering. "Oh, no. I'm not going to be here in the after-noon."

"Matt can't come over?" A look of horror crossed Tommy's face.

"No, I'm sure it will be okay." Trish patted his hand and prayed that the sixteen-year-old she'd hired to baby-sit wouldn't care if Tommy had a friend over. After all, it should only make her job easier. "I just need to check with Samantha. She's going to keep an eye on you while I'm at my in-terview. Isn't that exciting? Mommy may finally have a job."

Trish didn't tell him the job was in Kansas City. The way she looked at it, she needed to pay the bills, and the position had a lot of advantages: a rich benefit package, a salary equal to what she'd made in D.C. and a job description that sounded too good to be true.

Tommy's brows drew together. "Do you think Matt will bring his own ball?"

"I don't know, sweetheart." Trish smiled ruefully. She should have known better than to think Tommy would be excited about her news.

"If he doesn't," Tommy said, "we can use mine."

Her heart clenched. He'd been such a strong little boy, never complaining about her dragging him halfway across the country. But for the first time she could see how desperately he wanted a friend. Trish brushed a kiss across his forehead. "Do you know how much I love you?"

His face relaxed at the familiar question. It had become a nightly ritual. "Oodles and oodles?"

"That's right." She hugged him tight. "And don't you forget it."

Trish sat at her son's bedside until he fell asleep. She brushed a piece of hair back from Tommy's face. He was so young, so innocent. That long-ago night with Jack had changed the course of her life. But it had given her a great treasure.

Tommy had done okay so far, and if he missed having a father he never let on. Not telling Jack he was going to be a father had been the right decision.

But if Jack had loved her like she'd loved him,

Tommy would have had both a mother *and* a father.

Trish sighed. Why did she keep tormenting herself with thoughts of what might have been? This was the real world, not a dreamland with fairy-tale endings. A world where even if you loved someone, they didn't necessarily love you back. A world where you sometimes had to learn the hard way that Prince Charming could only be found in the pages of a storybook.

Chapter Four

"That boy is a real scrapper." Dan Cullen's voice was filled with admiration.

"He's got a lot of energy." Jack leaned back in one of the lawn chairs he'd confiscated from his mother's garage. "Makes me tired just to watch him."

"Don't give me that," Dan said. "You'd still be out there if my leg hadn't given me trouble."

For the past hour Jack and his brother-in-law had played a rousing game of two-on-two with the boys. Until the knee Dan had injured last year in a skiing accident had started aching.

"Believe what you want," Jack said, taking a sip of iced tea. He shifted his attention from his brother-in-law back to Matt and Tommy. Narrowing his gaze, he leaned forward. "Those boys are playing too rough."

Jack shoved his chair back and jumped to his feet just as Matt drove the ball down the court and slammed into Tommy.

Tommy's feet shot out from under him.

Jack crossed the driveway in three long strides but he wasn't quick enough to stop Tommy's fall.

"Tommy." Jack knelt down by the boy. "Are you okay?"

Tears flooded Tommy's eyes but he wiped them away with a grubby hand and nodded. Jack could tell the boy was doing everything he could not to cry.

"Is he hurt?" Matt leaned down, his freckled face filled with worry. "I didn't mean to knock him over."

"He's fine." Jack placed a reassuring hand on his nephew's shoulder, his gaze shifting to Dan. "But I think we've all had enough basketball for today."

"I think you're right. Matt and I have to get going, anyway," Dan said. "Julie should have dinner on the table by now."

"I'm really sorry, Tommy." Matt shifted awkwardly from one foot to the other. "Maybe when you feel better we can play again?"

Tommy bit his lip and nodded.

Jack waited until Dan and his son had driven off, before turning back to Tommy. He deliberately kept his voice matter-of-fact. "Your knee looks pretty banged up."

"It hurts." Tommy's voice quivered.

Jack's heart clenched. He hated to see anyone cry, especially a child. But showing undue sympathy might only make matters worse.

"I bet it does." Jack stared at the bloody raw area on the boy's knee. "But I'm afraid we need to get it cleaned up."

"That'll make it hurt more."

Jack met the boy's frightened gaze with a reassuring one of his own. "I'll be as gentle as I can."

Tommy stared at Jack for a long moment before he finally nodded and struggled to his feet.

The baby-sitter looked up when Tommy hobbled through the front door. Her eyes widened, and she gave a high-pitched shriek. "Oh, my goodness. There's blood running down his leg."

"That's usually what happens when you skin your knee," Jack said, shooting the girl a quelling glance.

"I'm not good with blood." Samantha chattered nervously as she followed them down the hall. "I fainted when we pricked our fingers in biology."

"You won't have to do a thing. I'll take care of it." Jack tried to keep the irritation from his voice. What was Patty thinking, hiring this child to watch her son?

Jack eased Tommy down on the closed toilet seat

before turning to Samantha. "You can go. I'll stay until his mother gets home."

Samantha hesitated. Jack could almost see her weighing her responsibilities as a baby-sitter with her desire to leave.

"He's an old friend of my mother's," Tommy piped up, repeating Jack's words from yesterday.

"Well, okay then," Samantha said with a relieved smile. She turned to go but stopped. "Tell Mrs. Bradley that she can drop by the money that she owes me tomorrow."

Jack reached into his pocket and pulled out a twenty-dollar bill. "Is this enough?"

"Wow." Samantha snatched the money from his fingers. "Yeah, this will do just fine."

"Bye, Samantha," Tommy said in a small voice.

The teen gave the boy a quick smile. "Be cool. And don't let him hurt you too much."

Jack stifled a groan. Once she was out of sight he picked up the soapy washcloth and met Tommy's apprehensive gaze. "This might sting, but we've got to get it clean."

"I know." Tommy expression was solemn. "But I can take it."

Fifteen minutes later, the large scrape had been cleaned, sprayed with Bactine and covered with a gauze pad that Jack had found in the medicine chest.

He'd just gotten Tommy settled in an easy chair

with a tall glass of orange juice when the front door swung open.

"Samantha, I'm home."

"We're in here, Mom."

Trish started through the parlor door and stopped short. Her gaze shifted from Tommy to Jack. Her breath caught in her throat. "What are you doing here? And where's Samantha?"

"She had to leave." The welcoming smile faded from Jack's face at her curt tone.

"Mr. Kreiger said he'd watch me." Tommy said quickly, and Trish could tell by his anxious tone that he'd picked up on the tension in the air. "That was okay, wasn't it?"

Trish crossed the room and forced a reassuring smile. "Of course it is, honey. It's just that you were Samantha's responsibility, not Mr. Krieger's."

"That girl was too young to be left in charge," Jack said.

"I think I'm a better judge of that than you are," Trish snapped.

"I have to disagree." He crossed his arms and his jaw tightened. "She might be okay if you're in town running errands..."

Her blood boiled. Who was he to insinuate she wasn't a good mother? That she didn't know what was best for her son? He hadn't been there for the 2 a.m. feedings or when Tommy had the chicken-pox. While he was attending fraternity parties, she'd been working and going to school *and* being a mother.

"...but she's not old enough to handle an emergency."

Emergency.

Trish's gaze shot to Jack's face, the words finally registering. "What emergency?"

His gaze shifted pointedly to Tommy, and for the first time she noticed the ice pack on his knee.

Trish rushed to Tommy's side. "Honey, what happened?"

"I fell." Tommy squirmed under her motherly concern. "It's no big deal."

"How did it happen?" Her accusing gaze shot to Jack.

Jack shrugged. "The boys ran into each other."

"The boys?"

"Matt Cullen," Tommy answered. "From swim class."

"I remember now." Her gaze shifted to Jack. "But that still doesn't explain what *you're* doing here."

"We played basketball," Tommy said, his face tense with worry. "It was fun."

"That's okay, sport," Jack said reassuringly. "Your mom is just trying to figure things out."

Before Trish could tell him that she could console her son, thank-you-very-much, he continued.

"Matt's father is my brother-in-law, Dan," Jack

said. "We thought it would be fun if we played a little two-on-two with the boys."

"I scraped my knee," Tommy said. "Mr. Krieger sprayed Bactine on it."

"How bad was it?" This time Trish kept her tone civil. Regardless of her feelings for Jack, it sounded as though he'd taken care of her son.

"Not too bad." Jack flashed Tommy a smile. "Though I think that leg may be sore for a few days."

"Sounds like no more ball playing for you," Trish said. "At least for a while."

"Aw, Mom." Tommy rolled his eyes. "It's not that bad. Can't Matt come over and…"

Trish frowned and Tommy's voice faltered.

"Patty…"

Trish shifted her gaze to Jack.

"I mean, *Trish*." Jack cleared his throat and shot her a smile. "Matt is a good kid. He didn't mean to hurt Tommy. It was just one of those boy things."

"Tommy is my son, Jack," Trish said firmly. "I'll decide who he plays with and when."

"But, Mom," Tommy whined.

She stopped the boy with a single glance. Sometimes Trish wondered if she was too strict with Tommy, but she'd seen too many single mothers lose control of their sons, and she was determined not to let that happen to her.

"I have no problem with Matt coming over,"

she said, directing the words to her son. "I'm just not sure it will work this weekend. I want to be completely unpacked and settled in before I start working, and I'm going to need your help. Can I count on you?"

Tommy reluctantly nodded.

"Did you get the job?" Jack asked. "Tommy told me you had an interview."

Though Trish wanted to tell Jack that her personal affairs really weren't any of his business, his question was probably more polite than nosy.

"I think I have a good shot at it," Trish said.

"Mom may be working at a bank," Tommy said.

"Really?" Jack's gaze sharpened. "What bank?"

Trish shifted uneasily at the gleam of interest in his eyes. "First Commerce in KC. They're expanding their PR Department."

"First Commerce?" Jack smiled. "My grandfather's friend is on their board. I'd be glad to ask Grandfather to have him put in a good word for you. Sometimes that's all it takes—"

"Thank you, no." Trish forced a slight smile. "I prefer to do this on my own."

"It wouldn't be any trouble," Jack said.

"I want to do this on my own," Trish repeated, keeping her gaze firm and direct. Though she wanted the job in the worst way, she didn't want Jack to be involved in any part of her life.

She'd made that mistake once.

Chapter Five

Trish hung up the phone, tempted to pinch herself to make sure she wasn't dreaming. Yesterday, First Commerce had told her they wouldn't make a hiring decision for several weeks. Today, the head of human resources had called, on a Saturday no less, and offered her the job.

For a brief second, she'd wondered if Jack had had a hand in this, but she'd immediately discarded the notion. They'd just talked last night. He wouldn't have had time to intervene.

The position was everything she could have wanted and then some. And the best part was, they wanted her to start right away.

Monday morning she'd report for orientation. That left this weekend to finish getting the house in shape, freeze some casseroles for dinner and... find a sitter for Tommy.

Her stomach tightened.

What if I can't find anyone? What will I do then?

Trish shoved the worry aside and reminded herself that there were bound to be lots of teenage girls who would love to earn extra money baby-sitting. She just had to find the right one. And she might as well start now.

Trish picked up the phone, dialed Samantha's number and crossed her fingers.

Half an hour later Trish heaved an exasperated sigh. Was everybody in Lynnwood at the ballpark? Tommy had told her the softball game between the high school seniors and the alums was a big event but she hadn't believed him. Until now.

Trish glanced at the clock. The game should be almost over. If she headed over to the ball field now, she might be able to find Samantha and ask her in person. At the very least she'd catch up to Tommy, who'd gone to the game with Matt and his family.

Still hopeful she'd have a baby-sitter before sundown, Trish headed out the door.

The bleachers were filled and the two teams were still playing when Trish got to the baseball field. She caught a glimpse of Samantha and her friends flirting with a couple of players and decided now might not be the best time to approach the girls.

Though she wasn't a big sports fan, Trish decided to watch the game and bide her time. She shaded her eyes with her hand and scanned the bleachers, finally spotting an empty seat halfway up on the end.

Trish climbed the steps, ignoring the curious glances. Even though she'd been in Lynnwood almost a month, she hadn't gotten out much. Though she didn't consider herself to be a coward, she'd found it awkward to meet people she'd once known who didn't recognize her; when they did, she often wished they hadn't.

Mrs. Russell, the checker at the A&P and no lightweight herself, had announced to everyone in line that "this girl used to be really fat and now look at her." The bank teller swore Trish couldn't be Mrs. Watson's granddaughter because that girl had been "positively huge" and not pretty at all.

Maybe it should have made her feel good about her appearance now, but it didn't. It embarrassed her to realize what everyone had been thinking and saying behind her back.

As if it were yesterday, Trish heard Jack's words and his friends' answering laughter: "As if I'd ever do anything with her." Her heart twisted at the memory.

The sound of a bat connecting solidly with a ball jerked Trish from her reverie. The crowd rose to their feet and roared their approval. Trish turned just in time to see Jack cross home plate. He was promptly mobbed by his teammates.

Trish shook her head and started back up the steps. How did the guy do it? Top of the ninth and Jack's home run had put his team ahead. He was the man of the hour. Again.

He'd always been popular. Valedictorian. President of the senior class. Football quarterback.

Trish heaved a heavy sigh and slid into the space at the end of the bleacher, smiling at the little girl sitting next to her.

"How are you?" Trish said.

"I'm three." The girl proudly held up three fingers.

"Kaela, the lady didn't ask how old you are." The woman smiled fondly at her daughter. "She asked how you are. Can you say fine?"

The girl ducked her head and shyly twisted a button on her bright-orange shirt. "Fine."

Trish smiled and her gaze shifted to the girl's mother. Now that she'd taken the time to really look at the woman, she realized she knew her. Trish quickly averted her gaze, but she wasn't quick enough.

"Didn't we go to high school together?" the mother said. "I'm Missy Campbell. Back then I was Andrews, Missy Andrews? Do you remember?"

Remember? How could she forget?

A knife twisted in Trish's heart. Popular with a

never-ending supply of friends, Missy Andrews had epitomized everything Trish wanted to be but wasn't.

"And you were...?"

"Patty Bradley," Trish said, feeling gauche and all of seventeen again.

Trish cursed the insecurity that made her stumble over her words and use her old name.

"Jack Krieger's neighbor." Missy smiled and nodded. "I thought that was you. But then I wasn't sure. You look so different."

"It *has* been ten years," Trish said lightly.

"You look fabulous," Missy said. "Nothing at all like the Patty I remember."

Trish forced a smile. "I go by Trish now."

"I like it." Missy said with an approving nod. "The name suits you. I'm thinking of dumping the nickname, too. Even though I still have a couple of years to go before I hit the big three-oh, I can't see myself as a thirty-year-old 'Missy'."

"I changed mine right after high school," Trish said. "When I lived in D.C. I was Trish. But here everyone still wants to call me Patty."

"Give 'em time," Missy said. "They'll come around. By the way, how long have you been in Lynnwood? I'm surprised I haven't run into you before now."

"We've been here a little over a month." Trish said.

"Did your husband get transferred back to the

area?'' Missy said with what sounded like genuine interest.

"No. It's actually just my son and me. It has been for a long time." Though Trish had been telling everyone for years that she'd married out of high school, got pregnant right away and then divorced, for some reason she couldn't make herself tell that old lie one more time.

"It's just Kaela and me, too." Missy tousled the little girl's hair. "Derek and I split up for good last year. We'd been living in Kansas City, but after the breakup I decided to move back. I wasn't sure how that would work out, but Jack and my other friends have been so helpful."

"Jack?" Trish's breath caught in her throat. She knew they'd dated in high school, so the fact that they were together now shouldn't surprise her. But it did.

"Jack Krieger?" Missy said. "I know the two of you weren't close, but don't tell me you don't remember him?"

"Remember who?"

A deep voice sounded beside her and Trish whirled.

"Hello, Trish," he said in a low voice, his gaze searching her eyes before shifting to her bare shoulders.

Her skin prickled.

"Uncle Jack." Kaela shot past Trish and wrapped her arms around Jack's knees.

"Hello, princess." Jack picked Kaela up and smiled. "You look like a pumpkin in that outfit."

The little girl giggled and Trish couldn't help but smile.

"She's been really good," Missy said, gazing at Jack with a fond smile. "We both screamed when you hit that home run. If I were in high school, I would have got up and led the squad in a cheer."

Trish resisted the urge to gag. And to think for a moment she'd thought Missy had changed. Trish stood. "I'd better get going. If I'm going to start work on Monday, that doesn't give me much time to get everything lined up, including a baby-sitter."

For a moment Jack's gaze narrowed, then a glimmer of understanding lit his eyes. "You got the job."

A smile stole across Trish's face, despite her best efforts to suppress it. "The head of HR at First Commerce called me himself this morning."

"Congratulations," Jack said. "That's wonderful. I knew everything would work out."

"Yes, congratulations." Missy stood. She moved closer to Jack and looped her arm through his. "Are you ready to go to the picnic? Kaela and I are both starving."

Though Jack didn't pull away, the puzzled look he shot Missy told Trish he wasn't sure what to make of her proprietary behavior. But Trish knew that Missy was staking her claim and telling Trish to back off.

Trish almost had to laugh at the thought of Missy Andrews being jealous of *her*. If anyone should be jealous, it should be Trish. But she wasn't. Because jealousy would imply she wanted Jack Krieger. And she didn't want him. Not in her life. And certainly not in her heart.

Jack waited until Missy and Kaela were safely inside their house before he pulled away from the curb. Though Lynnwood was a safe community, Missy had sworn her ex-husband had been following her when she'd been in Kansas City shopping last weekend. She'd been on edge ever since.

So when Missy had asked him in, he'd almost said yes. Until he'd seen the gleam in her eyes and realized her invitation had more to do with loneliness than fear of her ex-husband.

Missy knew as well as he did that she wasn't ready for another relationship. And, even if she was, he wasn't interested. She was a good friend and he adored her little girl, but whatever fire had once burned between the two of them had long since been extinguished.

His sister told him he was too picky and that if he wanted the large family he was always talking about, he'd better start seriously looking.

But it was easy for Julie to talk. She'd known since high school that Dan Cullen was the man for her. They'd married while they were still in college and they'd been together ever since. Jack wanted that same kind of love and if that meant he was too picky, so be it. He certainly wasn't going to worry about it. There were much more important things to think about.

His thoughts slipped back to Trish and how excited she'd been about her new job. Jack made himself a mental note to thank his grandfather's friend for his help.

Trish needed a break. Though she hadn't said much, Jack knew that losing her job in D.C. had been a severe blow to her confidence. Getting another job was a good first step toward rebuilding that confidence.

The next step was to find a sitter. When he'd mentioned Trish's new job to his sister, Julie had told him that most of the high school girls who baby-sat were booked months in advance.

Jack stopped at a light and decided he'd give Trish until tomorrow to find a baby-sitter. If she wasn't successful, he'd have to see what he could do to help her out. Whether she wanted him to or not.

"Do we have to go to church?" Tommy tugged at his tie. "Can't we just go out to eat instead?"

"We'll have lunch after church." Trish glanced in the car's rearview mirror and wiped a splotch of lipstick off her cheek. "Besides, we're already here."

"I bet your mother didn't make you go to church when you were my age."

"Actually, I wanted to go church," Trish said.

She'd been scarcely older than Tommy when she and her mother had moved in with Granny. And what she'd told Tommy was the truth. She *had* gone to church every week. Every week she would fold her hands, bow her head and pray that her mother's cancer would be cured and her father would come back.

Even after her mother had died, Trish had continued to pray. Until her grandmother told her that her father had remarried and was moving to California.

With his new wife.

Without his daughter.

Trish hadn't set foot in a church again until she'd found herself alone and pregnant with nowhere to turn. Over time she'd come to believe that everything happens for a reason. Because of moving to Lynnwood, she'd met Jack. Because of Jack, she had Tommy.

"I love you so much," she said abruptly, smiling at her son.

"Aw, Mom." Tommy had opened the car door, but he quickly pulled it shut. "It's okay to say things like that at home, but don't be saying it where someone might hear."

"Okay. I promise." Trish heaved a dramatic sigh. "But at least tell me that you love me, too."

"Mo-om." Tommy groaned and rolled his eyes.

"Or maybe I should open the door." Trish's hand moved to the latch. "Then everyone can hear…"

"I love you." Tommy's words came out in a rush, and a flash of red shot up his neck. "Okay, already?"

"Perfect." Trish flashed him a smile. "Let's go in."

For Tommy's sake Trish tried to act confident, but she'd worried how it would be, coming back to this tiny community church after being away so long.

But the moment she saw Pastor Williams, all her fears evaporated. His face broadened into a warm smile, and when Trish reached out to shake his hand, he hugged her instead.

"Patty Bradley." He held her at arm's length and studied her for a moment. "It is *so* good to see you. Welcome back."

Unexpected tears sprang to her eyes at the sincere greeting.

"And this must be your son." The minister's eyes shifted to Tommy. "Your grandmother told me all about you."

"Really?" A wary expression crossed Tommy's face. "What did she say?"

"She told me you liked sports." Pastor Williams's eyes twinkled. "We have a summer basketball league that practices down at the rec center on Thursday nights. We'd love to have you join us.''

"I don't know…'' Tommy's gaze dropped to his shoes.

"Matt Cullen's team could use another player.''

Tommy's head jerked up. "Matt goes to this church?''

"Yes, he does.'' Pastor Williams gestured toward the front of the church. "In fact, he's sitting with his family about halfway down, on the right.''

"I'm going to say hi.'' Tommy eagerly headed down the aisle, without so much as a backward glance.

"He's a wonderful boy, Patty.''

Trish didn't bother to correct him. She had a feeling she would always be Patty to him. And in his eyes, that had never been a bad thing to be. "I'm very lucky.''

"There was a time you didn't feel that way.''

"I know. But I've grown up a lot since then.'' Trish shifted uncomfortably from one foot to the other. "I hope you understand why I didn't come back for my grandmother's funeral. I wanted to, but Tommy and I were both sick with the flu—''

His hand on her arm stopped her words. "You don't need to explain. I know you would have been here if you could.''

"She died so quickly.'' Sometimes Trish had trouble believing her grandmother was gone.

"When she was out to visit last summer, she was doing great."

"None of us knew how sick she was," he said. "Until it was too late."

"I loved her so much," Trish said.

"You were the light of her life."

"That's nice of you to say, but..." Trish hesitated.

"But what?"

"I know my grandmother loved me," Trish said. "But I also know that I was a big disappointment to her. I was never pretty enough or thin enough or popular enough."

"Your grandmother wanted you to be happy. Sometimes she just pushed too hard." The minister's eyes filled with compassion.

"She did her best," Trish said simply.

"I'm glad you're back," the minister said. "If you need anything—"

"I know who to call." Trish smiled. "Now I'd better find a seat and let you get on with your work."

Though Trish would have preferred to sit in back, Tommy had already taken a seat next to Matt. Reluctantly Trish headed down the aisle, feeling the curious glances.

"I saved a spot for you, Mom." Tommy patted the pew. "Right here."

Trish took a seat and smiled politely at Matt's

parents. The organist had barely struck the first chord when someone tapped Trish on the shoulder.

"Is there room for one more?"

She turned in her seat. Jack stood in the aisle, looking every inch the successful businessman in his navy-blue suit and tie.

Tommy answered before Trish had a chance to say no.

"Sure, there's plenty of room."

The entire Cullen clan obligingly scooted down, and Trish had no choice but to move over.

Unfortunately "plenty of room" was an exaggeration. The space was barely big enough for a child, much less a grown man. When Jack sat down, Trish found herself wedged tight between him and her son. She hadn't been this close to Jack since that night in the closet.

Trish's insides turned weak and trembly, just remembering. Thankfully, when she picked up the hymnal to turn to the first song, her hands were steady. At least until he leaned closer.

"You smell terrific."

Trish shot him a censuring glance.

His smile widened.

She stared straight ahead.

He nudged her with his arm.

"Aren't you going to sing?" he whispered.

His tone was teasing, and she knew she should just banter back, but she couldn't. Her gaze dropped to the hymnal. This was too intimate. Sitting beside him in church. Sharing a hymnal. Their son at her side. His family close by.

Her heart clenched. This was the life she'd wished for, prayed for, dreamed of all those years ago. But it wasn't real, because the man beside her wasn't who he appeared to be.

If she had never overheard that conversation between him and his friends, she might have gone through life worshiping the ground Jack Krieger walked on.

But the scales had fallen from her eyes that long-ago prom night. She'd learned her lesson about what happens when love is blind.

Trish glanced sideways at the man beside her. No matter how charming, no matter how attractive, no matter how tempted, she wouldn't let herself be hurt again.

Chapter Six

The minute Pastor Williams finished the closing prayer and benediction, Trish grabbed her purse and popped up, her gaze focused on the nearest door. The last thing she wanted to do was to stick around and make polite conversation with Jack Krieger.

But in her haste to escape she'd forgotten that Jack stood between her and the aisle. When she made her move, he immediately rose to his feet and turned toward her.

"Good morning." The twinkle in Jack's eye told Trish he knew she'd been ready to bolt and had deliberately blocked her exit. "I was surprised to see you here."

"That makes two of us," Trish said. "I could

have sworn your family went to the Methodist church on Elm.''

''It closed,'' Jack said. ''About five years ago.''

''Closed?'' Trish frowned. ''I've never heard of a church closing.''

''The minister left. Membership dwindled.'' Jack shrugged. ''That was it.''

Trish started to ask why he'd chosen to attend this one, but thankfully she came to her senses just in time. She didn't want to talk to Jack a moment longer than necessary.

''Yeah, that'd be cool,'' Tommy said in an enthusiastic tone. ''We were going to eat out after church, anyway.''

Trish shifted her gaze toward her son, glad for the distraction. ''What's cool?''

''Matt invited us to have lunch with him and his family,'' Tommy said. ''Isn't that great?''

''I'm afraid—'' Trish thought quickly ''—that won't work. I have some errands I need to run—''

''But we were going to eat first, anyway,'' Tommy said, casting a beseeching glance at his friend.

''Puh-leeze, Mrs. Bradley,'' Matt said. ''We're having those big hot dogs and potato salad and everything.''

''It sounds delicious,'' Trish murmured. ''But—''

''My mom even baked a cake,'' Matt added. ''With chocolate icing.''

"Chocolate is my favorite," Tommy said. "Please, Mom."

Trish glanced from her son's pleading face to his friend's hopeful one. She wanted her son to have friends, and Matt was a great kid, but he was also Jack's nephew.

"We would really like it if you'd come." Julie Cullen had been talking to her husband, but she shifted her gaze to Trish and offered her a friendly smile. "I feel badly that you've been in town this long and we haven't gotten reacquainted."

"I don't want to intrude," Trish said.

"Julie makes enough food for an army," her husband chimed in. "You'd actually be doing us all a favor by saying yes. Otherwise we'll be eating leftovers all week."

Trish glanced at Julie and Dan. They'd never understand if she said no. "In that case," Trish said, mustering a smile, "I'd love to come."

"Great." Jack's voice sounded behind her and she realized with a start that he was still standing behind her. "Let's go fire up the grill."

"Fire up the grill?" Trish's heart sank to her feet.

"Didn't you know?" Jack said with an innocent expression. "Sunday's feast is at my house this week."

"You cook?" Tommy blurted out. The boy couldn't have looked more amazed if Jack had told him he could fly.

"You bet." Jack chuckled and ruffled the boy's hair.

"Is it hard?"

"Not at all," Jack said. "If you want, you can help me today and I'll show you how easy it really is."

"Sure," Tommy said immediately.

"Can I help too, Uncle Jack?" Matt asked eagerly.

"Of course you can," Jack said. He cast a questioning glance Trish's way. "I can use all the help I can get."

Trish lifted her chin and met his gaze with a cool one of her own. She had no intention of cozying up to a grill with Jack, today or any other day.

His lips twitched as if he found her reluctance amusing. "I'm parked out front. Why don't you ride over to the house with me?"

"No, thanks." Trish offered him a polite smile. "My car is in the parking lot."

"I know," he said. "But if you ride with me, it'll give us a chance to catch up."

"I'll drive myself."

"I'll bring you and Tommy back whenever you want."

Trish wasn't even tempted. She could easily see Tommy wanting to stay behind and play when the time came to leave. Then she would be alone with Jack during the car ride back.

"I'll ride with you," Tommy said, an eager smile on his face.

"That's fine with me," Jack said. "If your mom doesn't mind."

Tommy lifted his gaze to Trish. "It's okay, isn't it, Mom?"

No, she wanted to snap, it's not okay. She didn't want Tommy anywhere near Jack. But she held her tongue. Trish had learned long ago to pick her battles. And this, after all, was just a car ride. It wasn't as if Tommy was asking to go on a father-son outing.

"Trish?" Jack's voice rose in a question.

"Just make sure he buckles his seat belt," Trish said. Tommy let out a whoop. It was all Trish could do not to cringe.

Sitting beside Jack at church.

Having dinner at his house.

What would be next? Trish wondered.

She lifted her chin. Nothing would be next. Not if she had anything to say about it.

Because the farther she stayed away from Jack Krieger, the better off they'd all be.

Jack flipped the remaining burgers and turned down the flame. Between the kids' requests for more hot dogs and his grandmother's insistence that he prepare her chicken in a special way, he'd spent way too much time in front of the grill.

All he'd really wanted to do was talk to Trish.

But he'd been tied to the grill, and she'd managed to keep her distance. He had the distinct feeling she was avoiding him, which didn't make sense considering how close they'd once been.

In fact, they'd been the best of friends until the night of their senior prom. Guilt sliced through him. What happened in that storage closet had been his fault. But it hadn't been deliberate. God knew he'd never been the type of guy to take advantage of anyone. He'd never meant to steal her innocence.

Jack laid the spatula down and stared into the distance, remembering....

"Hey, look who showed up." Ron Royer let out a hoot. "And with a date, no less."

Chip Linderman shifted his gaze, but Jack wasn't even tempted.

"Old news," Jack said, straightening his cuffs. "I already saw Missy over by the coatrack ten minutes ago."

Jack wondered why he'd ever let Chip and Ron convince him to go stag. Sure, he'd been fighting with Missy, but they were always fighting. All he would have had to do was send her flowers and she would have been back in his arms in a heartbeat. But he'd wanted to show her he was tired of her petty games. He'd wanted to make a statement. But the joke ended up being on him.

Missy had a date. He had Chip and Ron.

"I'm not talking about Missy." Ron elbowed Jack and gestured with his head. "Take a look."

Jack shifted his gaze to the gymnasium's entrance, not because he was interested in who'd shown up, but because he knew Ron would keep at him until he did. His eyes widened. "Oh, my God, it's Patty."

"I knew you'd be surprised," Ron said with a sly grin.

"I can't believe it." Chip's eyes widened in amazement. "Even Fatty Patty has a date."

"Don't call her that." Jack narrowed his gaze. Who was Patty with? And why hadn't she told him she was coming tonight? "I don't recognize him."

"Obviously some nerd," Ron said in a dismissive tone. "Look at how he's dressed."

Jack's gaze drifted over the blue ruffled shirt Patty's date had worn with a tux.

"*She* looks okay," Chip said grudgingly.

Jack shifted his gaze back to Patty. Chip was wrong. Patty didn't look okay. She looked…beautiful.

In all the time he'd known her, Jack had rarely seen Patty in anything other than sweatpants and oversize T-shirts. But tonight, instead of being pulled back in a ponytail, her hair hung in loose curls to her shoulders. And though her dress didn't cling to her body like many of the dresses worn by the other girls at the dance, the green filmy folds flattered her curvy figure and brought out the emerald in her eyes.

The only thing missing was her smile. Jack noticed Patty's date seemed to have plenty of smiles...for everyone but her. When the guy left her standing alone to go over and talk to Kammie Parker, a girl who wasn't half as nice as Patty or half as pretty, Jack frowned.

"That guy's a jerk," Jack muttered. "Patty doesn't deserve to be treated like that."

"I never knew you cared." Ron's eyes gleamed.

Jack heard the unabashed interest in Ron's tone, and he knew he'd better watch his words. He forced a disinterested shrug. "She's my neighbor. That's all."

"I don't think that's all." Ron nudged Chip with his elbow. "I think Jack here likes the fat girl."

Jack gritted his teeth and remained silent, knowing it was the alcohol talking. Ron was a good guy but he'd "primed" a little too heartily before the prom and it showed.

"I think it's been so long since Jack got any, that even a heifer looks good to him," Ron continued.

Chip snickered and Jack shot him a glare. "You guys are talking crazy. I'm going to go and check out the babes."

"I told you he was horny," Ron said to Chip, and the sound of their laughter followed him across the gymnasium.

Jack wandered through the crowd, talking to friends, occasionally catching a glimpse of Patty and her date. Barely an hour after the dance started, Jack saw Mister Blue Shirt duck out the side door. Alone.

So he wasn't surprised when Ron stopped him later and said he'd stumbled across Patty crying in a hallway. Ron didn't bat an eye when Jack insisted on being taken to her.

Jack followed Ron to an area of the school so far from the gym he couldn't even hear the music.

"Are you sure she's way over here?" Jack slowed his pace, a sense of unease coursing up his spine.

"She didn't want anyone to see her," Ron said. He stopped in front of a large storage closet where the extra sports equipment was kept. "She's in there. Go ahead. Talk to her."

Jack hesitated. Something wasn't quite right, but he couldn't put his finger on it.

"Jack, is that you?" Patty's voice sounded from inside the room.

Casting aside his sense of foreboding, Jack stepped into the room. Patty stood back by a stack of boxes, an anxious expression blanketing her face.

He moved quickly to her side. "Are you okay?"

She blinked. "I was going to ask you the same question."

"You were?" Jack said. "Why?"

"Ron told me you needed to talk to me," she said, pushing a strand of hair back from her face. "He was quite adamant about it."

Suddenly it all made sense. Jack turned, but he wasn't quick enough. The door slammed shut in his face. Laughter erupted from the other side.

Jack reached for the knob, only to discover it was locked from the outside. His fist hit the door with a resounding thud. "Ron! This isn't funny!" Jack yelled. "You let us out of here."

"You two have a good time." Despite the heavy oak door, Jack recognized Chip's voice. "See you in the morning."

"In the morning?" Jack kicked the door. "The hell with in the morning. You open this door now!"

Silence greeted his tirade and Jack realized that he and Patty were alone. Stuck in a storage closet. And knowing his friends, he had the sinking feeling it would be morning before they'd be back. But he'd never been one to give up easily.

"If we make enough noise, someone is bound to hear us," he said to Patty, who stood wide-eyed, with her back pressed up against a pile of boxes.

"I don't think so." She shook her head. "This room is too far away from everything. We could yell and scream all we wanted and it wouldn't make a bit of difference."

"How can you be so calm?" Jack raked his hand through his hair and paced. "Don't you realize we could be here all night?"

"I know," Patty said with a resigned sigh. "But what can we do about it?"

"Your grandmother is going to have a stroke if you don't come home tonight."

"Actually she's in St. Louis for the weekend. Her sister got out of the hospital today and needed some help." Patty plopped down on a stack of exercise mats. "She won't be back until tomorrow night. But what about your mom?"

"I'm spending the night at Chip's house—" Jack gave a little laugh. "Or rather, I was."

Patty's unblinking gaze searched his face. "Why do you think they did it?"

Jack paused. Though he didn't know for sure, he had a sneaking suspicion why Chip and Ron had locked them in the closet together.

"They're just being drunk and stupid," he said, as if that said it all.

Patty gave a rueful grin, accepting his explanation without comment. "I wish they'd picked a cleaner place."

Jack grimaced at the sight of Patty's beautiful dress now streaked with dust. "I'm sorry about all this. I hate it that they ruined your evening."

"It wasn't going that well, anyway." Patty lowered her gaze to the floor. "I never even got a chance to dance."

Though her words were matter-of-fact, Jack's heart clenched at the pain in her voice. "That guy was a fool."

"You're right about that." Patty lifted her gaze to meet his, her green eyes large and luminous. "What kind of guy agrees to go on a blind date to a prom? He should have known a girl with a "great personality" would be fat and ugly."

"Don't say that." The pain in her eyes tore at Jack's heartstrings. "I meant he was a fool to ditch you. You're beautiful."

A flush stole up Patty's face. "Yeah, right."

"You are," Jack said. "And before the night is over, you're going to have that dance."

"It's a nice thought, but it's not going to happen." Patty gestured to the surrounding shelves. "We've got balls and bats and plenty of floor mats, but not a band in sight."

Jack smiled. Obviously, she didn't know a little thing like that would never stop a Krieger. "We'll make our own music."

He extended his hand to Patty. She stared doubtfully for a moment, then took it and let him pull her gently to her feet. But once she was standing, he didn't let go. Instead he drew her close, surprised at how natural she felt in his arms.

Though they'd spent almost every Friday and Saturday night of the past year together, they'd never touched. So he was unprepared for the surge of emotion that hit him when Patty laid her head against his shoulder.

A clean scent of vanilla wafted about him, and

without thinking he nuzzled her hair, inhaling deeply. "You smell wonderful."

She shivered.

Jack stepped back. "Are you cold?"

He considered offering her his jacket but when he searched her eyes, the smoldering jade he found there was anything but cold.

"I'm not cold at all," she said.

Patty licked her lips and Jack had the overwhelming urge to taste them, to discover for himself if they were really as soft as they looked.

Suddenly Jack's tux felt too hot and too tight. He gave a nervous laugh. "Good, when you shivered, I wondered..."

"I'm not cold," she repeated, her hand tentatively touching his arm. "Not at all."

Jack, who was never at a loss for words, simply stared. Was she saying what he thought she was saying?

As if in answer to his unspoken question, Patty lifted a hand to his face. When she spoke, her voice was low and husky. "May I kiss you?"

He focused his gaze on her face. "I'd like that."

Without a second thought to the wisdom of his action, Jack lowered his lips and met hers halfway. He kissed her slowly and lingeringly, discovering in the process that her lips were indeed as soft and sweet as they looked.

When that kiss ended, he kissed her again. And again. This time her mouth opened, and the kiss deepened. His breath grew ragged and his heart pounded in his chest. He'd kissed a lot of girls but this was different. Fire burned his veins, and suddenly kissing wasn't enough. His hand cupped her breast, his thumb teasing…

"Jack?" Trish's voice sounded in his ear.

Startled, Jack jerked back, and the spatula went flying. His heart hammered against his chest.

"Are you okay?" Trish automatically reached down to pick the utensil up from the thick grass.

"Boy! You get out of that tree. You're going to fall and break your neck!" Grandma Irene's voice split the air.

Trish's gaze darted to where Jack's grandmother stood in the middle of the yard, shaking one bony finger in the direction of a tall oak tree.

Her gaze settled on her son, twenty feet in the air and still climbing. The wind, which had been nonexistent when they'd gotten out of church, now caused the leaves to flutter and the branches to sway dangerously.

Like a mother lion, Trish let out a roar. She sprinted across the yard, her heart in her throat, scarcely conscious of Jack matching her stride for stride.

"Tommy!" Trish yelled. "Stop!"

Tommy ignored her and grabbed a higher branch.

Anger replaced the fear. "John Thomas Bradley. You better stop this very instant."

Trish rarely used her son's full name, reserving it for only the most serious of circumstances. Thankfully it had its desired effect.

Tommy paused and gazed down. "I can't come down now, Mom. Oreo needs me."

For the first time, Trish noticed a small black-and-white cat on the branch directly above Tommy.

"That blasted cat," Jack muttered under his breath.

"I'm sure the kitty can get down on his own," Trish said in her most persuasive tone.

The boy didn't budge.

"Tommy, Oreo doesn't need your help. She climbs that tree all the time," Jack said. "She'll be fine. You need to do what your mother says and come down."

Trish held her breath.

Tommy's gaze shifted from the cat sitting on a branch just out of his reach licking a paw, back to Jack. "Are you sure?"

"Positive," Jack said.

By now the entire family had gathered beneath the tree, including Matt who'd come sauntering out of the house, a Popsicle in each hand. "What's going on?"

"Your friend decided to climb a tree." Though Jack spoke to his nephew, his gaze remained focused on Tommy. "Know anything about it?"

"He's in the tree?" Matt's gaze lifted. "Wow. He's really high."

Trish shivered, and Jack patted her shoulder. "He'll be fine. I used to climb all the way to the top when I was a kid."

The words had barely made it past Jack's lips when Tommy slipped. A collective gasp rose from the group. Trish grabbed Jack's forearm, her nails digging into his skin.

For a moment the boy dangled in the air, his hands grasping the big branch in a precarious grip. In what seemed like minutes, but could only have been seconds, Tommy found his footing.

Trish kicked off her heels. "I'm going up after him."

"No, you're not," Jack said. "I am."

She whirled. "I'm his mother. I can take care of him."

"I know you can." Jack's gaze met hers. "But I'm stronger than you."

Though Tommy was only nine, he was a big kid. If he lost his footing, Trish wasn't sure she *would* be able to hold him.

"Okay." Trish spoke with quiet, but desperate, firmness. "You go. Just don't let him fall."

"I won't." Jack whipped off his chef's apron and shoved it in Trish's hand. "Trust me."

The words sent a chill up her spine, but what choice did she have? Her eyes remained glued to Tommy, and she scarcely breathed as Jack made his way to the boy. Though it seemed like forever, in only minutes her son was safely on the ground.

Trish hugged Tommy until he squirmed. After he ran off to play with Matt, with stern instructions not to go near any more trees, Trish went looking for Jack. She found him in the kitchen, restocking the refrigerator with soda.

He looked up when she entered, then straightened, wiping his hands against his pants as she crossed the room to stand beside him. "Did you need something?"

"I need to say thank you," she said softly. "I can't tell you how much I—"

Jack's mouth curved in a slight smile and he pressed a finger to her lips. "You don't have to thank me. I was glad to do it."

His touch sent a tingle of electricity coursing through her, and Trish stepped closer, relief and gratitude short-circuiting her normal reserve. Her hands rose to rest on his shoulders, and she impulsively brushed his cheek with her mouth.

She'd intended it to be an impersonal thank-you kiss. A kiss you'd give a brother. Or a friend of your grandmother. But Jack turned slightly and she met his lips. And instead of pulling away, her arms wrapped around his neck.

It was an exquisite kiss. He caressed her mouth more than kissed it. And when his tongue swept across her lips with tantalizing persuasion, she opened her mouth to him. In the heat of the moment she didn't pause for even a second to consider the ramifications of kissing Jack this way. In fact, as Jack unhurriedly claimed her mouth, drinking her in, Trish stopped thinking at all.

She met each thrust of his tongue with equal passion until shivers raced down her arms and chest, settling in her breasts. She pressed herself against him with wanton abandon.

He shifted, and she could feel the hardness of him, straining against his khakis. She heard a groan and wondered, in the fog of desire, if it came from his lips or hers.

She met his gaze and caught her breath at the raw hunger in his eyes. For a split second she gave in to the fantasy that he truly did want her, that maybe he even loved her.

"Oh, Patty," he whispered, his breath hot against her ear. "What you do to me."

Patty?

He tilted his head, ready to kiss her again, but she jerked back, her heart pounding in her chest.

"Jack, I need more—" Julie paused in the doorway, her gaze shifting from Jack to Trish, her eyes bright with curiosity. "I hope I didn't interrupt anything."

"Not at all," Trish said, resisting the urge to straighten her clothes. "In fact, I was just leaving. Tommy and I need to get going. Tomorrow is a big day."

"Trish—"

"Thanks for the hamburgers—" Trish interrupted Jack, then turned to Julie "—and for everything. It was great."

Before anyone could stop her, Trish made her getaway. The last thing she wanted to do was talk to Jack about what had happened.

What had she been thinking? How could she have so easily forgotten that valuable lesson he'd taught her so long ago? No matter how much she wanted to believe otherwise, she had to remember that happiness would never be found in Jack Krieger's arms.

Chapter Seven

Jack sat back in the kitchen chair and took a sip of iced tea. His Monday had been busy but, inexplicably restless, he'd left work early. Instead of heading straight home, he'd made a quick detour to his sister's house. "How's the baby-sitting going? Sorry you said yes?"

"Not at all." Julie smiled. "Tommy's a good kid. And watching a nine-year-old doesn't take that much work."

"Eight."

"What?"

"Tommy's eight, not nine," Jack said.

"You're wrong." Julie lapsed into that superior know-everything-older-sister tone that had always rubbed him the wrong way. "The boy is nine."

"Eight." Jack smiled. "But if you want to believe he's nine…"

"We'll settle this right now," Julie said. She stood and crossed the kitchen, opening the screen door. "Tommy, could you come in here a minute?"

Moments later both Tommy and Matt burst into the room, their smiles widening at the sight of Jack.

"What's up?" Matt grabbed two cookies from the plate Julie had set on the table and handed one to Tommy.

"Tommy, didn't you tell me your birthday was in February?" Julie asked.

"Nope." Tommy swallowed the bite of cookie he'd just shoved into his mouth. "It's in January."

Jack shot his sister a confident smile. He couldn't wait for her to eat crow. "And how old are you?"

"Nine," Tommy said. "I'm older than Matt."

"Just by a few months," Matt protested.

"I'm still older."

"Boys." Julie clapped her hands, effectively stopping the squabble. "Now that you've had a snack, why don't you go out and play while you have the chance. It won't be long before Tommy's mother is here."

To Jack's surprise, the boys didn't argue. They each grabbed a couple more cookies and scurried out the door.

"So, was I right or what?" Julie said.

"He can't be nine," Jack said. "That's all there is to it."

"Jack." Julie shot him a smug glance. "The boy is nine. You were wrong. Just admit it."

"But it doesn't make sense," Jack said. "If he was born in January, that would have meant Patty, I mean Trish, got pregnant in high school."

"So?" Julie raised a brow. "She wouldn't have been the first girl at Lynnwood High to find herself in that situation. Though come to think of it, I don't think I ever saw her on a date."

"I did once," Jack said, thinking back to that long-ago night. "She came to the prom with a date."

"Bingo," Julie said. "That's when it happened. The dates are perfect."

"They are, aren't they?" A band tightened around Jack's heart until he could scarcely breathe. Dear God, had Patty gotten pregnant from their one night together? But she said she'd been married. Even Pete had said she was divorced. There had to be a logical explanation. Patty never would have kept such a secret from him.

His mind raced, searching for an explanation. There had been no guys before him, that he knew. But what had happened after she'd left Lynnwood was a mystery. She'd been young and vulnerable, but he couldn't believe she'd have jumped into bed with the first guy she met.

Jack shoved back his chair. "I need to get going."

"Why don't you stay for dinner?" Julie said, clearing off the table. "We're having pot roast."

Though he hadn't eaten much for lunch, the thought of food turned his stomach. "I'm not hungry."

"Since when has that ever stopped you?" Julie laughed. "When you were younger, Mom and Dad used to joke that your stomach was a bottomless pit. You'd eat a big meal, say you were full, then polish off a whole pie for dessert."

"You're making that up." Jack said.

"John Thomas Kreiger," Julie said with mock seriousness. "God is listening to you lie to your sister."

She continued to scold him in a teasing way but Jack barely heard her

John Thomas.

A knot formed in the pit of his stomach. He moved to the window and stared out at the dark-haired boy shooting hoops. Tommy couldn't be his son. He just couldn't.

Could he?

Trish eased the car next to the curb in front of Julie's house and shut off the engine. She leaned back against the headrest for several moments and let herself relax for the first time since she'd stumbled out of bed at 5 a.m.

She'd been awake most of the night. The memory of Jack's kisses had taken center stage in her thoughts and made sleep an impossibility.

She wondered if Tommy was in the mood for takeout. Though she'd wanted to start the week out right by making a nutritious meal, at this moment the thought of pizza was infinitely more appealing. If they ate off paper plates, her cleanup would be reduced to tossing the box in the garbage.

With her meal plans finalized, Trish got out of the car. She strode up the sidewalk, riffling through her purse in search of an elusive pizza coupon. She was halfway up the front steps before she saw Jack sitting on the porch swing.

Her steps faltered. A hot flush stole up her neck.

"Jack. What a surprise." Trish forced a casual tone. "I didn't expect to see you again."

He raised a dark brow.

"I mean tonight." She stumbled over the words. "We need to talk."

"I'd love to." The lie slipped quickly from her tongue. "But I'm afraid I'm running late. Another time perhaps?"

He rose from the swing and in a few strides crossed the distance between them to stand in front of her. "Now. Not later."

Trish lifted her chin. She had no intention of discussing her crazy behavior. She was tired. She was hungry. But most of all she was embarrassed.

"I told you, I can't right now," Trish said. "Tommy needs his dinner—"

"He's eating even as we speak," Jack said. She started to interrupt, but he held up a hand. "I told Julie it would be okay. I told her you and I had something we needed to discuss."

"We have nothing to discuss." Trish took a step back before the intoxicating scent of his cologne addled her senses. "And you have no right to make decisions concerning my son."

"Don't I?" He met her gaze with an enigmatic look. "Are you sure about that?"

"Very sure." Trish reached for the screen door.

"So sure that you're willing to go inside and risk having everyone, including Tommy, hear what I have to say?"

Something in Jack's tone made her pause.

"Okay." Trish lifted her shoulders in a casual shrug. "Since it's such a big deal, I suppose I could spare five minutes. Just say what you have to say."

Jack shook his head. "This conversation needs to be private. It's your choice. We can walk to the park or go to my house."

Choice? She'd be alone with him either way, unless there were some other people at the park....

"Let's go to the park," she said. "But we'll have to keep it short. Your sister has had Tommy all day."

"Let's go," he said, heading down the steps. "I want to get this over with."

Suddenly it made sense. He wanted to apologize for his behavior last night and he didn't want anyone to hear. Obviously, she wasn't the only one who was embarrassed.

Her tension eased. Maybe it was best to get this out in the open. Then there wouldn't be this horrible awkwardness when their paths crossed in the future.

Her step picked up and by the time they reached the park, Trish felt almost lighthearted.

"This one looks clean." Jack gestured to a stone bench inside the gazebo.

"Looks fine to me." Trish brushed the stone surface with her hand before sitting down. The blue suit she'd worn today was her favorite and she wasn't about to get it dirty. "What's up?"

Jack blew out a ragged breath and met her gaze for a long moment. "I feel like such a fool."

Trish's shoulders slumped in relief. It was a good start. At least they both agreed they'd behaved foolishly. Though she knew he'd enjoyed the kisses as much as she had, they'd been playing with fire. And they couldn't allow it to happen again.

She cleared her throat. "I think we both let our hormones override our good sense."

He frowned. "What are you talking about?"

"Last night in the kitchen," she said. "What are you talking about?"

"I'm talking about Tommy," he said. "About him being my son."

A chill filled Trish's body, and her blood froze in her veins. She forced herself to breathe. "Tommy? Your son? Where'd you ever get such a crazy idea?"

"The dates are right," Jack said, his words clipped and his voice tight with strain.

"What do you mean?" Trish stalled for time.

"We made love in April," Jack said. "Tommy was born in January."

This was the very thing Trish had worried about when she'd decided to move back to Lynnwood. Thankfully she'd planned for this contingency and had come up with a plausible story. The question was, could she pull it off?

"Tommy was premature," she said. "He came almost three months early. The doctors said it was a miracle that he lived."

Something flickered in Jack's eyes. "So you must have met Tommy's father—"

"Right after I moved to Washington," Trish said. "I was new to the city and so was he. We were both lonely. I think that's why things moved so fast."

Jack let out the breath he'd been holding. There *was* a logical explanation after all.

But what about the name?

"Why did you call him John Thomas?" Jack asked. "That name has been handed down in my family from father to son for five generations."

"Tommy's father split before he was born." A

pink flush tinged Trish's cheeks. "I'd always liked the name John Thomas, and I couldn't think of anything I liked better… I hope you don't mind."

"No. I completely understand." Jack moved to her side and awkwardly patted her shoulder. "I can't tell you how stupid I feel."

"I bet you're also relieved," Trish said.

"In a way," Jack admitted. "But Tommy's a great kid. If I did have a son, I'd want him to be just like him."

His gaze lingered on Trish. Her hands lay tightly folded in her lap, and a thin sheen of perspiration dampened her forehead.

Jack reached over and squeezed her hand. "Thanks for being honest with me."

He knew it'd been hard for her to admit that she'd married the first guy that asked, but he was glad she'd told him the truth. Because honesty had always been important to him. And if their relationship turned into something serious, he certainly didn't want any lies between them.

Trish tucked Tommy into bed and gave him a hug. "Do you know how much I love you?"

"Oodles and oodles," he said with a smile.

"That's right," she said, kissing his forehead. "And don't you forget it."

She turned on the night-light before pulling the door closed. Tommy was such a good kid. She'd been truly blessed.

If I did have a son, I'd want him to be just like Tommy.

Jack's words followed Trish all the way to the kitchen. She poured a tall glass of milk and took a seat at the table.

Had she been wrong not to tell him? After all these years, the denial had been automatic. She'd vowed long ago never to have any ties to the man who'd broken her heart with his lies, learning the hard way how appearance could be deceiving.

Trish's thoughts drifted back....

Patty snuggled up against Jack, his bare skin warm and smooth against hers. Though a storage closet wouldn't normally be considered a romantic hideaway, Patty couldn't remember when she'd been so happy.

"We'd better get dressed." Jack pushed up from their "bed" of drop cloths and reached for his pants.

She grabbed his wrist and pulled him back down beside her. "What's your hurry?"

He brought her hand to his lips and nibbled on her fingers until she giggled. "It's almost six and I don't want to take the chance of someone surprising us."

It made sense, but the night had been so wonderful, so magical, that Trish hated to see it end. She rolled over, her breasts brushing against his chest, her fingers weaving their way downward through the hair on his belly.

"Oh, Patty." In one swift movement Jack pulled her on top of him. "What am I going to do with you?"

She smiled and met his gaze, the look in his eyes a mere reflection of her own need. "I've got a few ideas."

They made love again and, as Jack caressed her, it took all her willpower not to cry out her love for him. She desperately needed to hear him say it first. But as the words remained unspoken, she consoled herself with the thought that sometimes actions speak louder than words. And over the next hour he'd shown her in more ways than she'd thought possible, how much he cared.

Afterward they dressed in silence, smoothing their rumpled clothes and exchanging shy smiles. Even with his hair mussed and a stubble of whiskers on his cheeks, Jack still looked incredible. She knew a dozen girls who would kill to be his girlfriend. Patty still couldn't believe he'd chosen *her*.

"I can't believe it's morning already." Patty ran her fingers through her hair, suddenly nervous. "Last night it seemed like tomorrow would never come, and now it's here...."

Jack captured her hand in his, stopping her chatter. "Last night was great. I want you to know—"

Laughter sounded from the hall and the doorknob jiggled. Jack dropped Trish's hand like it was a hot potato and moved from her side just as the door opened.

Ron and Chip strutted into the room. They wore jeans, T-shirts and broad grins. "You guys have fun?"

"Yeah, it was a blast," Jack said, his voice filled with sarcasm. He gestured to the drop cloths lying near his feet. "You try sleeping on a concrete floor."

The boys talked for a few minutes, during which time Jack didn't so much as glance her way. It was as if she'd ceased to exist. Her heart twisted. It was almost as if last night had meant nothing to him at all.

"I'm going to the rest room." Patty brushed past them, tears suddenly pushing at the back of her lids.

After freshening up, she padded down the hall, her stocking feet making no sound on the shiny linoleum. At the end of the hall Jack stood talking with his friends, his back to her.

"What do you mean by that crack?" Jack's voice carried down the silent hall. "I have a girl-friend. You know that."

Ron mumbled something, then he and Chip laughed.

"You're crazy." Jack stiffened. "As if I'd ever do anything with *her*."

For a second Patty foolishly thought he was talk-ing about Missy. Until she heard her name. And Chip and Ron laughed again.

Patty's stomach lurched and her knees started to tremble. For a moment she thought she would faint. But after a couple of steadying breaths, she regained her composure.

She told herself she should have known better than to think Jack cared. He'd wanted sex. She'd been convenient. And willing.

God, how willing she'd been. How wanton. Her cheeks burned red-hot remembering her actions. She'd practically begged him to make love to her...and in every way possible.

Patty blinked back her tears and straightened her shoulders. By the time she reached the boys, her eyes were dry.

"I need to get my shoes," she said to no one in particular.

"I'll give you a ride home," Jack said.

"Don't bother," Patty said, proud she could sound so offhand while her heart was breaking. "You've had to put up with me all night."

"I don't mind—" Jack said.

"Jack, my man, let the girl walk." Ron glanced at Patty's round figure with undisguised disdain. "God knows she could use the exercise."

"That's enough," Jack snapped.

Though Ron's insensitivity was nothing new, his comments still hurt. But at least she knew where Ron and Chip stood. Far more dangerous were people like Jack. People who pretended to be your friend. People who said one thing to your face, but laughed at you behind your back.

"Ron's right." Patty lifted her chin. "I need the exercise."

"Let me give you a ride," Jack repeated. "It's the least I can do."

Her nails dug into her palms. She bit back a sharp retort. "Thank you, no. You've already done quite enough."

Patty held her tears until she was back in her own room, in her own bed. She slammed her fist into her pillow again and again until sobs racked her body.

How could she have been so stupid?

Her own father hadn't loved her.

Why had she ever thought a guy like Jack would?

"Mom?"

Trish's gaze jerked to the kitchen doorway, and she blinked trying to get her bearings.

"Are you okay?" A frown marred Tommy's forehead, and his blue eyes were filled with concern.

Trish exhaled a shaky breath and wiped her eyes with the back of her hand. "I'm fine, honey."

"But you were crying."

"When Mommy gets tired, sometimes she just feels like crying," Trish said in a matter-of-fact tone. "Then I'm all better."

Tommy's suspicious gaze narrowed. "Do you feel better now?"

"Actually I do." Trish realized as she said the words that they were true. Reliving that awful time had made her realize she'd been right not to tell Jack that Tommy was his son.

Jack was a charmer. A man who could make a woman forget her good sense with a flash of a smile. But Trish was an adult now not a naive girl, and Tommy's welfare was her number-one concern. She wanted her son to grow up to be a good man. One who would never leave his family when times got rough or make love to a girl and then cast her aside.

All those years ago, Jack had shown he couldn't be trusted. So Trish would be foolish to trust him with her son.

Or with her heart.

Chapter Eight

"Tommy's looking good," Jack said. "That was a great save."

Trish looked up in surprise. She'd been coming to Tommy's softball games for two weeks, and this was the first time she'd run into Jack. Actually it was the first time she'd seen him since he'd asked if Tommy was his son. "What are you doing here?"

"I came to watch the game," he said. "Here, hold this."

Jack handed her a large soda and set his lawn chair down next to hers on the edge of the ball field.

"No, really," Trish said. "Why are you here?"

"Be-cause," he said with a heart-stopping grin. "There was someone here I wanted to see."

For the briefest of moments, Trish fantasized that

it was her he'd come to see, until his gaze slid over to where his nephew was warming up on the sidelines.

Of course. He'd come to watch Matt play. She handed him back the plastic tumbler. "Here."

Jack put his hand around the cup, but didn't pull it from her grasp. "Want a drink?"

"No, thanks. I don't drink soda."

Jack shrugged and took the drink from her. "My sister doesn't like the taste, either."

"The taste is okay." Trish leaned back and stretched her legs out before her. "It's the calories I don't like."

"You don't look like you need to worry about it," he said.

"Yeah, right," she scoffed. "I'm a regular beauty queen."

Today, she'd rushed getting ready and had simply pulled her hair up in a ball cap, put on a tank top and a pair of khaki shorts and called it good.

His gaze roved and lazily appraised her scantily clad body. "You look pretty beautiful to me."

Her skin prickled beneath his gaze. Trish lifted her chin and resisted the urge to cross her arms across her chest.

"I've missed seeing you," he said softly. "I would have called but—"

"You don't owe me an explanation." Trish shifted in her chair and gave a little laugh.

Jack paused for a moment, clearly nonplussed.

"Well, even if you didn't miss me," Jack said, "I missed you. In fact, I was wondering if you and Tommy would like to go to Kansas City with me tonight. We could have dinner? Maybe catch a movie?"

"I'm afraid Tommy has a birthday party, actually a sleepover, tonight," Trish said.

"What about you?"

It was the unsure look in his eyes and the fact that she *had* missed him that stopped Trish from lying and saying she had plans. Anyway, what would be so wrong with spending the evening together?

"A movie does sound kind of fun," she said. "Do I get to pick which one?"

He bantered with her about the movie during the rest of the game and on the ride to drop Tommy off at his party. It wasn't until they'd reached Kansas City that he gave in and let her have her way, rolling his eyes when she picked a "chick flick."

But afterward, when he wanted "something sweet," she let him choose the place. He picked a gourmet ice-cream parlor in a quaint little building in Country Club Plaza.

"I thought you loved ice cream," Jack said, glancing from his chocolate marshmallow sundae to her small dish of vanilla. "That's why I wanted to come here."

"I do love it," Trish said taking a tiny spoonful from her dish. "I'm just a little more careful than

I used to be. Back in high school I'd eat a big bowl every night. I don't do that anymore.''

''You always did have a healthy appetite,'' Jack said.

''Back then food was my way of coping with life,'' Trish said.

''It had to be hard,'' Jack said, his spoon paused in midair. ''Losing your mother when you were so young.''

''You can't imagine.'' Trish set her spoon down and leaned back in her chair.

''I remember you used to tell me how much you missed her,'' Jack said.

''Being an only child, she wasn't just my mother, she was my best friend. When my dad left, it was bad. But when my mother died...'' Trish swallowed hard against the lump in her throat. ''I'd never felt more alone.''

''You had your grandmother.''

''Yes, I did,'' Trish said. ''And she did the best she could, given the circumstances.''

''Circumstances?''

''She was an old lady who should have been playing bridge instead of raising a teenager. I know she wanted my father to be more involved, but he wasn't interested.'' Trish shifted her gaze and blinked. ''By the time my mother died, he had a wife and a baby on the way. So my grandmother was stuck with me. I tried to stay out of the way.

I studied a lot, helped her around the house and…I ate. Food became my best friend.''

"I knew it was bad, but I didn't know it was *that* bad." Jack reached across the table and took Trish's hand. "I'm sorry you had to go through all that."

Tears pushed at the back of Trish's lids. She took a deep breath. "What do they say? That which doesn't kill us makes us stronger?"

Jack squeezed her hand before releasing it. "Still, I wish I could have been there for you."

"You were," Trish said, realizing it was true. "All those nights we sat and talked on my grandmother's porch meant a lot to me."

"You're being kind," Jack said. "Looking back I don't think I was a very good friend to you."

"Why do you say that?"

His gaze dropped to his sundae, his handsome face serious. "For one, I knew you missed your mother but I never even invited you over so you could get to know mine."

"Your mother already had a daughter," Trish said. "She didn't need another one."

"Still—"

"Jack, really," Trish interrupted. "Don't give it a second thought."

"I'm sorry," he said. "I really am."

"Like I said, it's okay."

"It's not okay," he said. "I want to make it up to you."

"Make it up to me?" Her brows drew together. "What are you talking about?"

"I want you to give me another chance to show you what a good friend I can be," he said. "We'll start over. This time I won't let you down."

Fool me once, shame on you. Fool me twice, shame on me.

Trish stared into the guileless depths of his eyes and wondered if she was crazy to even consider his offer.

But didn't everyone deserve a second chance? And, anyway, she'd be on her guard.

He wouldn't fool her again, because this time she wouldn't let him.

"I don't know why Jack couldn't have come with us," Tommy said for what had to be the hundredth time. "He likes roller coasters, too."

Even though Worlds of Fun had just opened for the day, the parking lot was already filled with cars. The sun shone overhead and the blue sky promised a beautiful day. Trish pulled into the next available parking place.

"I've already told you." Trish tried to speak calmly and ignore the irritating whine in Tommy's voice. "This is *our* special time. Jack has his own life. We have ours."

"But he could—"

"Tommy, stop! Not another word."

Tommy's eyes widened and Trish took a deep

steadying breath. There was no need to get so up-set. Just because Jack hadn't called in over a week was no reason to snap at her son. Julie had told her he'd been out of town, but Trish knew for a fact he'd returned yesterday. She'd seen his Jeep parked by the bank on Friday.

But she wasn't going to think about that now. She was going to concentrate on having fun with her son. All week long she'd tried to keep up with the cleaning and laundry so on Saturday she could concentrate on Tommy. They'd gotten up early so they'd have a full eight hours at the popular Kansas City amusement park.

"We're going to have a great day." Trish forced a bright smile. "I might even ride the roller coaster. What do you think about that?"

"But you always throw up," Tommy said. "When we went to Six Flags you threw up all over that man—"

"I'd just eaten," Trish said, her stomach already churning at the memory of that horrible last ride. "And cotton candy and roller coasters are never a good combination."

Trish saw no need to mention that the two times before that, she'd ridden on an empty stomach and had still gotten sick.

An hour later Trish stood facing a formidable foe: the Orient Express. The winding structure looked even scarier close up, and the screams from the riders sent chills up Trish's spine. Her heart picked up speed and perspiration dotted her upper lip.

"Wow," Tommy said. "This will be great. Let's go get in line."

"Are you sure you want to wait?" Trish said, trying her best to stall. "That line looks pretty long."

"It'll move fast." A familiar masculine voice sounded behind Trish.

"Jack!" Tommy whirled, a bright smile blanketing his face.

Trish turned slowly, her heart fluttering in her chest. "What a surprise."

"I know." Jack chuckled. "Who'd ever think we would run into each other here?"

Certainly not Trish who'd dressed super casual in jean shorts and a Redskins T-shirt. While Jack, in his khaki shorts and navy polo shirt, looked as if he'd just stepped off the pages of *GQ*.

"You're looking lovely as ever," Jack said with an appreciative smile.

Trish could barely resist rolling her eyes. In the rush to get ready, she'd only used the minimum of makeup and pulled her hair back into a ponytail. Lovely? Hardly.

"Jack, are you sure you want to go on this thing?" Missy hurried through the crowd, an iced fruit drink in one hand. She stopped short. "Why, Trish. What a surprise."

Trish wished she could sink into a hole. Despite

the heat, Missy looked cool and fresh in a lemon-colored shorts outfit with strappy sandals. Dark strands of her perfectly cut hair softly brushed her shoulders.

"Missy. How nice to see you." Trish shoved aside her embarrassment and smiled. Her gaze scanned the nearby crowd. "Is Kaela with you?"

"She was supposed to be," Missy said. "But then she got sick last night. My sister is watching her for me today."

You left your child when she's sick?

Trish bit back the words. Though she'd never left Tommy when he was ill, she knew many people didn't have such reservations.

"My mom always stays home with me when I'm sick," Tommy said. "Don't you, Mom?"

"Well, I…" Trish hesitated.

"One time she even missed a big test," Tommy said. "I had a high fever. It was 108."

Jack's lips twitched.

"More like a 104." Trish put a hand on Tommy's shoulder, her touch softening the correction. "You were a pretty sick boy."

"Kaela didn't have a fever," Missy said. "Well, maybe just a little one. But that's pretty common with ear infections."

"I'm sure your sister will take good care of her," Trish said.

"I know she will." The tension in Missy's face eased. "I knew you'd understand, being a single mom and all. Jack and I have had this trip planned for a long time. I didn't want to cancel."

"But it was more for Kaela than us," Jack said. "I told you I'd understand if you wanted to stay home with her."

"But I didn't *want* to cancel." Missy linked her arm through his. "I'm so tired of spending my weekends at home doing nothing. Though I'm not really sure I want to spend it riding this monster."

Missy lifted her gaze to the overhead track and pretended to shudder.

"I love roller coasters," Tommy said. "They're awesome. Mom promised this time she'd go with me."

Jack smiled at the boy before his gaze shifted to Trish. "I didn't think you liked roller coasters."

"She hates 'em." Tommy answered before Trish had a chance to open her mouth. "Last time she puked all over this bald guy. He was so mad. You—"

"Tommy." Trish put a hand on her son's shoulder and gave it a squeeze. "That's enough."

Jack's smile widened.

"If he wants, he can ride with me." Jack cast a sideways glance at Missy. "Unless you really want to go."

"I'll give up my seat gladly." Missy laughed and waved a dismissive hand. "You two go ahead. Trish and I will just sit in the shade beneath that tree over there and relax. Come and find us when you're done.''

''Have fun,'' Trish said, but Tommy was already chattering happily to Jack, and she didn't think he even heard her.

Trish and Missy exchanged smiles and headed over to the nearby bench.

''Want a sip?'' Missy held out the fruit drink.

Trish shook her head. ''No, thanks.''

Over the next half hour, Trish and Missy talked about everything and everyone...except Jack.

Finally, Trish couldn't stand it any longer. Even though it was none of her business, she had to know what was going on between Missy and Jack. So when Missy mentioned Jack's name, Trish jumped on it.

''So are you two serious?'' Trish said in what she hoped was an offhand tone.

Missy didn't answer immediately. She took a sip of her drink, her gaze focused in the distance. Finally, just when Trish had started to wonder if Missy was going to answer at all, she spoke.

''I'm just getting out of a bad marriage, a really bad marriage.'' Missy's voice was tight with strain. ''It's way too early to think about getting serious with anyone. But if I ever do decide to take the big step again, I can see it being with someone like Jack. He's the best. But I'm sure you already know that.''

Trish just smiled. She knew most people in

Lynnwood would agree with Missy. Jack had a reputation for being a hardworking businessman, a dedicated community volunteer and, as Missy had said, an all-around great guy.

Maybe, given the chance, he would even be a good father.

"Do you believe people can change?" Trish asked abruptly.

A tiny frown marred Missy's brow. "In what way?"

"Let's say a person is selfish and self-centered when they're young. Do you think a person like that can change? Or do you think those characteristics are part of that person's basic personality?"

"I believe people can and do change." Missy paused for a long moment. "Some for the better. Some for the worse. Over time, people show their true colors. You just have to give 'em rope to either redeem or hang themselves. Take my ex for example. He had a temper when we dated, but as the years went on he got just plain mean."

Her mind wandered as Missy chattered on.

The woman had given her a lot to think about. Maybe Jack wasn't the same self-centered guy who'd broken her heart. Tommy certainly adored him. But before she let Jack become more a part of her son's life, she would do as Missy suggested and spend more time with Jack. Get to know him better. See if he really had changed. After all, what did she have to lose?

Chapter Nine

"I'm glad you called." Trish daintily wiped her mouth with the paper napkin. "This pizza hits the spot."

"With Tommy at the church camp-out this weekend, I thought you might like some company." Jack smiled. "After all, what would you do with all that time to yourself?"

"I think I could find something," Trish said with a wry grin.

Jack couldn't help but think again how pretty she looked this evening. Though her sundress wasn't particularly short, it showed a fair amount of cleavage and a lot of honey-colored skin.

Ever since Jack had picked her up, all he'd wanted to do was touch her. When he'd opened the car door and she'd brushed past him, he'd wanted to take her in his arms right then and there. But this evening was about renewing their friendship, not kissing.

And Trish was a great conversationalist. It had been a long time since he'd laughed so much. But between the enticing scent of her perfume and the sensual way her tongue licked the last bit of pizza sauce from her lush lips, he was having difficulty concentrating.

"It's nice having the chance to get to know each other again." Trish said, fiddling with her straw. "Of course, we knew each other in high school, but people change."

"I don't think we've changed that much. We still enjoy spending time together, just like we did when we were eighteen," Jack said.

"If you enjoyed being with me so much back then, why didn't you ever ask me out?" Trish leaned across the table, her eyes glowing with a curious intensity.

The question took Jack by surprise. To say he'd never thought of asking her out would sound ridiculous. Unfortunately it was the truth.

He took his time chewing, stalling for time.

"Were you ashamed of being friends with me?" she pressed. "Is that what it was about?"

"No," he said. "Of course not."

"Then why didn't you ever introduce me to anyone as your friend? Why didn't we ever go out on a real date?"

After all these years, Jack wasn't sure why it mattered to her, but he could tell it did. Jack shifted uncomfortably in the red vinyl seat.

"Actually," he spread his hands out in front of him and decided he might as well be honest, "I never thought of it."

"You never thought of it?" Trish arched a disbelieving brow.

"It's true." Jack leaned forward, doubting he could make her understand something he didn't quite understand himself. "I had my friends. I just assumed you had yours."

"Yeah, well…" Trish shrugged.

Shame filled him at the thought of how he'd failed her. "I'd do anything if I could turn back time."

They sat there in silence for a long moment. Jack couldn't help but wonder how his life would have been different if he'd let Trish be a real part of his life back then. Would she be his wife now? Tommy, his son?

"We can't turn back the clock but we could start over," Trish said.

Jack thought for a moment, the idea fraught with endless possibilities.

"I like the idea of starting over," Jack said at last. "Tonight could be a new beginning for us. Sort of like a first date."

"What about last week when we went to dinner and a movie in Kansas City?"

"Okay, this is our second date," Jack said, warming to the idea.

Trish agreed, and after finishing off the rest of the pizza, they headed over to Lynnwood Lanes for some "moonlight bowling."

It quickly became apparent to Jack that Trish was no pro. When she almost ended up down the alley with her ball, Jack insisted on putting his arms around her to do a little "coaching."

Unfortunately his advice didn't help. Trish couldn't keep the ball from the gutter. But she didn't seem to care. And neither did Jack. He liked teasing her and he especially liked having her in his arms. It seemed they'd barely started when the game was over.

"Maybe I should be glad we weren't together back then," Trish said with a grin, untying her bowling shoes. "You're kind of a wild guy."

Jack winked at her. "You ain't seen nothing yet."

She giggled. They dropped off their shoes at the counter and headed to the car.

"I had a great time, Jack," Trish said with a pleased smile. "If this is what dating in high school was like, I'm sorry I missed it."

"The night is still young." Jack opened the car door for her and smiled. "We still have another stop."

"Really?" Trish's eyes widened in surprise. "It's almost midnight. What else in town is open?"

"It's not in town," Jack said, shutting her door. He whistled as he rounded the Jeep and got in the driver's seat. "We're going to Grogan's Point."

He slipped the key into the ignition and backed up.

"Are you serious?" Trish said. "Everyone knows that the only reason you go to Grogan's Point is to make out."

"You're right," Jack said. "Back then it was *the* place to go."

"Is that where you took Missy?"

Jack glanced at her curiously. "A few times. But I was usually in such a hurry to see you, that Missy had to settle for a kiss or two at the door."

"Settle for?" Trish's lips twitched.

Jack smiled modestly and turned his attention back to the highway. At the next corner, he turned off the asphalt and onto a gravel road.

"You're serious," Trish said. "You're really going to take me there?"

He cast her a sideways glance. "Unless you don't want to..."

"No. We can go there." Trish straightened and stared straight ahead, her cheeks bright pink. "I've never been up there at night."

Jack shifted gears, anticipation coursing through his body. What was that saying of his mother's? The one that seemed to fit this moment?

Ah, yes. "The best is yet to come."

He smiled and his foot hit the accelerator.

* * *

With her fingers laced behind her head, Trish stared idly up at the sky. She'd wondered what Jack had in mind when he'd opened the door and pulled a blanket from the back. But when he'd explained that he knew a grassy area off to the side that would give them a better view of the stars, she'd released the breath she hadn't realized she'd been holding.

They sat there for a while and talked, but when Jack suggested that they lie back and relax, her heart had once again picked up speed.

But so far, all they'd done *was* relax. And, of course, look at the stars.

"Penny for your thoughts," Jack said softly, breaking the silence.

Trish could feel the warmth traveling up her neck, and she was grateful for the darkness. "I was wondering what the big deal was about coming up here."

"You don't like it?" Jack raised himself up on one elbow.

Trish shrugged. "It's okay. But it's kind of boring."

"Oh, now I understand." Even in the dim light Trish could see the gleam in his eye. "The lady wants some action."

Without another word, Jack's arm slipped over Trish. He pulled her close.

Trish giggled, feeling like a schoolgirl again. She

snuggled up to him and breathed in the scent of him.

"Is this better?" His voice sounded low and husky against her ear.

"Hugging is nice," Trish conceded.

"Nice?" Indignation rang in Jack's voice, but she instinctively knew it was all for show. "This is our first date. I was trying to be polite."

"It's our second date. And you don't have to be *that* polite," Trish said, the desire to feel his lips on hers making her bold. "You can kiss me if you want. I wouldn't mind."

"You don't have to ask twice," Jack said.

"I didn't ask—"

Jack's lips smothered her words, and Trish decided it didn't matter who'd asked, because she'd gotten what she wanted.

His lips were warm and sweet against her mouth, and Trish relaxed in his arms, savoring the closeness. He kissed her as if they had all the time in the world.

She'd become an expert over the years at keeping men at arm's length, but spending time with Jack this evening had made her realize how much she'd missed the companionship. Her breath caught in her throat at the thought of how much she'd missed *him*.

Trish tilted her head back, reveling in the sensation of Jack's mouth on her neck.

"Are you still bored?" His husky whisper brought a smile to her lips.

"Maybe just a little." She lied straight-faced, gazing at him through lowered lashes. "This is pretty tame stuff."

Jack stared at her for a long moment, before his large hand cupped her face and his gaze met hers.

"I want to do it right this time," he said softly. "I don't want to rush."

What Jack said made sense. But she'd spent the last ten years away from this man. And now he was back, stirring her emotions with a kiss and a gentle caress. Maybe it didn't make any sense, but, basking in the golden warmth of his touch, being with him had never seemed so right.

"Who said anything about rushing?" she whispered. "We have all night."

His gaze traveled over her face and searched her eyes, until a tiny smile lifted his lips. "You're right. We have all the time in the world."

Reclaiming her lips, he crushed her to him.

Burying her hands in his thick hair, Trish opened her mouth to his persuasive probing. They kissed until Jack's breath was hot against her cheek. Until her breasts strained against the thin cotton fabric of her dress. Until all she wanted was him.

Almost as if he could read her thoughts, Jack's hand slid inside her dress and cupped her breast. She wiggled against his touch, reveling in the long-forgotten sensations. When she thought she would die with longing, his thumb rubbed across the swollen tip and Trish arched back, the ache inside her now a fiery need.

Jack smiled. With the flick of a finger he pushed aside the fabric, and his head bent to follow the path of his hand.

Trish couldn't stop herself from shuddering, or from responding to the feel of his mouth on her skin.

His hand moved lower...

"They've got to be here somewhere," a man's voice said.

Jack's hand froze and Trish stiffened.

"Fool kids." The voice sounded from the direction of the car.

"You got a flashlight?"

Panicked, Trish's gaze shot to Jack.

Dear God, there wasn't just one man, but two.

Jack put one finger to his lips, and they slowly sat up. She straightened her dress and ran her fingers through her disheveled hair, her heart pounding in her chest.

Jack smoothed the blanket and gave her hand a reassuring squeeze just as two deputies came into the clearing.

The flashlight beam briefly settled on Trish before shifting to Jack. "Why, Jack Krieger. I saw the Jeep, but I didn't realize it was yours. I didn't expect to see you here."

"I didn't expect to see you here either, Fred,"

Jack said with a laugh. "Trish and I came here to get a better view of the stars. I hope there's not some kind of law against that?"

"Of course not," Fred said. "But most of the people who come up here are kids. And most of them have more on their minds than looking at the sky."

"It's the truth," the younger deputy chimed in. "In fact, last week we came upon this couple bare-ass naked and—"

"Howie!" The older officer frowned. "That's confidential police business."

"It's hard to believe," Jack said. "Doing something like that in such a public area."

Heat rose up Trish's neck at the thought of how exposed she'd been only moments before.

Fred chuckled. "You get those hormones going and I swear people will do it anywhere."

"Hard to believe," Trish echoed. She wondered how far she and Jack would have gone if the deputies hadn't shown up when they did.

"Well, sorry to disturb you." Fred touched the brim of his hat. "You two enjoy the rest of your evening."

Trish waited until the men were out of sight before she spoke. "As soon as they leave we'd better go, too."

Jack's gaze met hers. "You sure you don't want to look at the stars a little while longer?"

"Wanting isn't exactly the problem," Trish said.

She remembered the vow she'd made sitting alone in that tiny apartment all alone with a new baby: no sex before marriage. All these years it hadn't been difficult to keep that vow…until now.

"No, it isn't." Brushing a kiss across Trish's lips, Jack stood and then helped her up.

"Where do we go from here, Jack?" Trish brushed the wrinkles from her dress with the palm of her hand.

"I'm going to take you home. Like I said, we don't have to rush." Jack looped his arms around her shoulders. "I like you, Trish Bradley. This time we're going to do this right."

This time we're going to do this right.

Trish removed the breakfast dishes from the table, unable to believe how much had changed since the night he'd first voiced those words.

They'd been taking it slow, getting to know each other again. When Tommy had ball practice, Jack would meet her at the field and they'd watch the game together. On the weekends she and Jack would take in a concert or a movie.

Though there was no secrecy about their relationship, Trish doubted anyone in Lynnwood knew they were dating. Though he was affectionate in private, after that night in the bowling alley, he'd never so much as held her hand in public.

Her doubts were confirmed when Trish ran into Missy at the grocery store, and the woman made a special point of mentioning that she needed to give Jack a call so they could "get together."

Trish had bitten her tongue. How could she say Jack was already taken when there was no real commitment? After all, there had been no talk of marriage, and her ring finger was bare.

Trish stared down at her left hand. What would she say if Jack asked her to marry him?

Over the past few weeks Jack's behavior had swept aside most of her reservations. Though she'd never be able to understand how he could have once been so callous, she firmly believed the man had changed.

The front screen door slammed shut. Seconds later Tommy burst into the kitchen.

Trish smiled at the excitement on her son's face. "What's up?"

"I got a letter." Tommy held up an envelope. "All the way from Washington."

Trish lifted a brow. "Who's it from?"

"Peter," Tommy said, his gaze slipping back to the envelope.

Peter Wessel had been Tommy's best friend since preschool. When they'd first moved to Lynnwood, Tommy had talked constantly about his old friend back in D.C. But once Tommy and Matt had become friends, he'd scarcely mentioned Peter.

"You got something from Washington, too." Tommy tossed her a legal-size envelope.

Trish caught it in one hand and flipped it over, expecting to see another bill.

Carlyle Consulting.

Her heart skipped a beat. The well-respected Washington consulting firm had been her top choice when she'd been on her job hunt. Though they'd expressed interest and had even interviewed her, at the time she was looking they hadn't had any open positions.

There had been a message on her recorder from someone in their office last week. She hadn't gotten around to calling them back.

Trish broke the seal and lifted the flap of the envelope, quickly reading the enclosed letter.

Her eyes widened. She read the words again and gave a strangled laugh.

"What is it, Mom?" Tommy's face filled with concern. "Is something wrong?"

"No, not at all." Trish shook her head, unable to believe the irony. Three months ago she would have jumped for joy at such an offer: twice her old salary with a generous car allowance to sweeten the pot. "It's just a job offer from one of the places in D.C."

"We're not going back, are we?" Tommy said, a worried frown edging his brows. "I like it here."

"I do, too." Trish smiled reassuringly. She carefully folded the paper and slipped it back into the envelope. Later, when she did her bills, she would type a quick note declining the offer. The position wouldn't even start until after Labor Day. The company had plenty of time to hire someone else. "We're not going anywhere."

Why should she? Lynnwood was her home, and everything she'd ever wanted was right here.

Chapter Ten

"But I thought you said you were free this Saturday." Trish forced herself to stay calm knowing that overreacting would accomplish nothing.

"I know I did." Jack took a bite of the sandwich Trish had fixed him for dinner and chewed for a moment. "But that was before Larry Ketterer backed out of being the emcee for the chamber of commerce's annual dinner."

"But why do *you* have to be the one to do it?" Trish hated to press, but they'd had plans to get together with some of her co-workers for weeks, and she'd been looking forward to it.

"Goes with the territory." Jack shrugged and took a sip of iced tea. "I'm the immediate past president of the chamber."

His gaze softened, and she knew he saw through

her attempt to hide her disappointment. He pushed aside his plate. "I can't tell you how sorry I am. I was looking forward to meeting your co-workers."

Trish's heart hung heavy in her chest.

"I'm sure they'll understand," he said, when she didn't speak.

"I know they will," Trish said. "But I wanted you to get to know them a little before the big golf outing."

"When is that again?"

"A week from Saturday." An uneasy sense of alarm slid up her spine. Trish straightened in her chair and met his gaze. "You're still planning to go, aren't you?"

"Wouldn't miss it for the world." Jack smiled reassuringly. "I can't wait to meet your friends."

Appeased, Trish relaxed. For one brief moment her old insecurities had surfaced, and she'd wondered if he was trying to avoid being seen as her "date."

"You'll never guess who I saw at the bank." The chime of the clock in the hall reminded Trish that Tommy needed to start getting ready for ball practice. "Ron Royer."

"Is that right?" Jack paused. "How's he doing?"

Trish narrowed her gaze, surprised Jack sounded so indifferent.

"Okay, I guess," she said. "I mean, he seemed pleasant enough. We talked for a few minutes. He and his wife live in Overland Park. They have two little boys.''

"So he and Jane are still together," Jack murmured.

"If you want, maybe we can all get to—"

"I don't think that would be a good idea," Jack said, cutting her off. "Ron and I were friends in high school. But that was a long time ago."

Though it didn't make sense to Trish, she let the subject drop. After all, Ron had never been a favorite of hers, anyway. So what did she care if Jack didn't want to socialize with him? All that mattered was that Jack was still coming to her company's golf outing.

It would be their first big event as a couple. Unless he meant for her to go to the chamber of commerce dinner with him?

Trish hesitated, hating the fact that even after all this time she still felt so unsure.

"So, is this thing with the chamber a bring-your-date kind of event?" Trish tried to keep her tone casual and offhand as if it didn't matter one way or the other to her. "If it is, it wouldn't be a big deal for me to cancel my plans. That is, assuming you wanted me to go?"

Jack shifted in his seat. "I'd love for you to come with me. But since I'll be the emcee, we wouldn't have much time together, anyway, so you might as well go ahead and keep your plans."

"I wouldn't mind," Trish said in a light tone.

"It might be kind of fun. You know, eat some rubbery chicken and make fun of the emcee."

She flashed him an impish grin.

"You're obviously a connoisseur of such events." Jack chuckled.

"Seriously, if you'd like me to go, I will."

"You're such a good sport." Jack reached across the table and took her hand. "But I won't ask you to give up a night with your friends for something like this. It's bad enough that I'm bailing out on you."

Disappointment settled like a leaden weight in the pit of Trish's stomach. Didn't he want her to go with him? She gazed at him, unable to tell for sure.

"The only bad thing about going with my friends is that it's sort of set up to be a 'couples' event." She waited once again for Jack to invite her to the chamber dinner, but he remained silent.

"I guess I could get one of the guys at work to go with me," Trish said, filling the awkward silence. "Someone said Joe in accounting might be interested in...in coming."

Jack's jaw tightened, and Trish felt an absurd sense of satisfaction. She waited for Jack to protest, to mention something about them being exclusive, to say he didn't want her dating other men, even if it was just Joe from accounting.

Instead Jack took another sip of his tea and met her gaze. "It's always good to get to know people from other areas of the company. Why not ask him?''

Trish stared at Jack for a long moment. ''Why not indeed.''

Instead of going back to the bank after leaving Trish's house, Jack headed home and pulled the lawn mower out of the garage. It only took two times around the perimeter to convince him that he'd definitely gone crazy. What other explanation could there be for his actions?

Mowing the yard in ninety-degree heat with 80 percent humidity made about as much sense as encouraging the woman you loved to go on a date with another guy.

Jack stopped dead in his tracks, wondering why the realization that he'd fallen in love with Trish Bradley was such a shock. She was everything he'd ever wanted in a woman.

Why, then, had he given his blessing when she'd mentioned going on a date with Joe from accounting?

Because it wasn't a date, he told himself. Any more than it was a date when he and a group of co-workers went out for drinks on Friday afternoon. Besides, although Trish had put on a brave face, he could tell how much going out with her friends meant to her.

No, he'd done the right thing in encouraging her to be with her friends. Last time their relationship had been all about him. He wasn't going to let that happen again.

When he was sure she was ready to hear what he had to say, he'd tell her how he felt about her. And about Tommy. Because he knew they were a package deal. And that was okay with him.

Tommy was a good kid. A boy any man would be proud to call his son.

"Jack."

The unexpected sound of his name pulled him from his reverie. He turned and eased down the mower's throttle to a soft growl.

Missy stood at the sidewalk's edge, looking surprisingly cool in a white sundress sprinkled with tiny blue and yellow flowers. She beckoned to him with one hand. "Could you come over here a minute?"

Relieved to have an excuse to stop, Jack shut off the mower and ambled across the yard. "What's up?"

"Great news." Her appreciative gaze traveled down his body before rising to his face. "I'm going to the chamber dinner tonight. Instead of my father."

"Really?" Jack wiped the sweat from his brow with the back of his hand. Missy's father had been one of the founding members of the Lynnwood Chamber of Commerce and Jack couldn't remember the last time the man had missed a meeting, much less the annual dinner. "Where's your dad going to be?"

"He and my mom left for Denver this afternoon," Missy said. "My sister just had her baby."

"Be sure and tell her congratulations for me." Jack hadn't even known Missy's sister was pregnant. "Isn't Jenny's husband in the military?"

Missy nodded. "He's over in Croatia...or some place like that. So my parents went to help her out. They'll probably stay a couple of weeks. Derek wasn't much help when Kaela was born, but he was better than nothing. I can't imagine doing it alone."

An image of Trish flashed in Jack's mind. It must have been hard for her, being a teenager, alone in a big city with a premature baby.

"So I was wondering if that would work for you?" Missy stared at Jack with an expectant gaze.

Jack tried to keep his face impassive. "Maybe."

"Maybe?" Missy's brows drew together. "What kind of crazy answer is that? Either you can give me a ride to the dinner or not."

"Of course I'll pick you up," Jack said smoothly. "Tell me again why you need a ride?"

"Be-cause." A hint of exasperation crept into Missy's tone. "My car is in the shop getting the brakes fixed, and I don't want to walk a mile and a half in heels."

"Don't get all riled up," Jack said with a laugh. "I said I'd take you."

"What about Trish?"

Jack frowned. "What about her?"

"Word is that you two are an item," Missy said, her eyes bright with interest. "Are you sure she won't care if I tag along?"

"Trish isn't coming," Jack said.

"Really?" Missy's gaze grew sharp and assessing. "Don't tell me you two broke up already?"

Irritation rose inside Jack and his voice came out sharper than he'd intended. "Did I say that?"

"Not in so many words." Missy lifted a finely arched brow. "But if you're together, then why isn't she coming to the dinner with you?"

"Be-cause." Jack mimicked her earlier response. "She's got plans with friends in Kansas City."

"Kansas City." Missy pretended to shudder. "Glad it's her and not me."

"What's wrong with KC?" Jack said. "When you were in high school, you practically lived at the Plaza."

"It's definitely lost its appeal." Missy lifted a shoulder in a slight shrug. "Every time I go there now, I get this creepy feeling, like Derek is just around the next corner."

"You were okay when we went to Worlds of Fun."

"That's because I was with you," she said. "And because I remembered how much Derek hated the place."

Though Missy tried to make light of it all, tiny lines of tension edged her eyes.

"Is he still threatening you?"

"You mean am I still getting calls from all those pay phones? The ones the police say they can't do anything about?" Missy brushed back a strand of hair with a dry laugh. "Every week."

"Have you seen him?"

She shook his head. "Not in months. Not since that time he followed me all around Kansas City. I keep expecting him to show up here. I hate having my parents gone. I don't trust him. Not one bit."

"At least you have the restraining order," Jack said. The last time Missy had seen her husband face-to-face, she'd ended up in the hospital.

"A lot of good that'll do." She snorted. "Believe me, if Derek wants to get to me he will, restraining order or not."

"If he comes around, call the sheriff."

"Fred?" Missy gave a humorless laugh. "Get real. The guy is great at rescuing cats from trees and breaking up parties, but he's hardly one to count on in a crisis. Howie isn't much better."

She cleared her throat and shifted her gaze.

Her manner was nonchalant, but Jack could see fear behind the tightly held control. It showed in the tremble of her hands, the look in her eye and the catch in her throat. Though she was trying hard to be brave, Jack knew how badly she'd been shaken by that last encounter with her husband.

What kind of man would hit a woman? Jack could never tolerate such behavior, and that's why he'd ended his friendship with Ron Royer. Why Ron's wife continued to stay with the guy was beyond Jack's understanding. But until Ron was willing to admit he had a problem and get help, Jack didn't want anything to do with him.

"I'll get by," Missy said. "It'll all work out."

Jack wondered if she was trying to convince him or herself. He met her gaze.

"If you ever need help," Jack said, "I want you to call me."

"You have your own life," Missy said. "I can't expect you to drop everything just—"

"Anytime," Jack said firmly, cutting off her protests. "You have my cell number. If you need help, you call. Understand?"

"You're sure you wouldn't mind?" Missy searched his gaze as if looking for any hint of hesitation. "It would just be while my father is out of town...."

"Missy." With two fingers under her chin, Jack tipped her face up. "You and I are friends. If you need me, call me. It's as simple as that."

"Okay," Missy said at last. "But could you do me a favor?"

"Depends," Jack said, with a teasing smile, trying to lighten the mood.

"Could you not say anything about this to your sister? Or to anybody?"

"Why?" Jack said, his expression sobering. "It's nothing to be ashamed of."

"I know." Missy's gaze shifted down to her feet. "But it's still embarrassing."

"If that's the way you want it." Jack patted her awkwardly on the shoulder. He didn't understand, but he'd respect her wishes.

"Thank you so much for everything." Missy leaned forward, her rosy lips slightly puckered.

He expected a kiss on the cheek, an impersonal kiss from one friend to another.

Instead, she planted her lips firmly on his and wrapped her arms around his neck.

Startled, he let her finish the kiss before he stepped back, extricating himself from her hold. "What was that for?"

"For being such a good friend," Missy said with a little smile. "You never used to mind when I'd kiss you."

"That was a long time ago," Jack said.

Missy stared at him for a long moment. "Yeah. B.T."

"B.T?" Now she had him completely baffled.

"Before Trish. It's funny when you think about it," Missy said with a rueful grin. "In high school I had it all. Trish had nothing. Now she's the one who has it all."

Jack stared at her in disbelief. Obviously he wasn't the only one acting crazy today. "You have Kaela. You have your friends and your family. You call that nothing?"

"I know, you're right." Missy paused for a long moment.

"One of these days you'll find someone who deserves you. Someone who loves you as much as I love Trish."

"I gave up hoping for my own Prince Charming long ago." Missy heaved a sigh. "But you're as close as I ever got, and I have to tell you I'd hoped you'd still be available when I was ready to start dating seriously again."

Jack just smiled and shrugged. He and Missy had known each other long enough that if anything were meant to come of their relationship, it would have already happened. She had to know that as well as he did.

No, it was he and Trish who were meant to be together. All he had to do was be patient until Trish discovered that for herself.

Chapter Eleven

The porch swing creaked as Trish bent over, putting the last coat of polish on her toenails. The evening breeze caressed her cheek and she reached up with one hand to brush back her hair.

Instead of going out as she'd planned, Trish had spent the evening with her son making pizza and playing board games. Though she'd experienced a momentary twinge of uncertainty when she'd cancelled her plans with her co-workers, Tommy's joy at hearing she was staying home with him wiped away that doubt in an instant.

Tommy had definitely been psyched. Trish paused, remembering how her son had pumped his fist in the air when he'd beaten her at Monopoly. Though he was looking more like a young man every day, in that moment he'd been just an excited little boy. One who, when bedtime came, begged for an extra hour even though he could barely keep his eyes open.

He'd been asleep before his head hit the pillow. Trish smiled. Though she and Tommy had their moments when they butted heads, she wouldn't trade her son and her life with him for anything.

At eighteen all she'd been able to see was the bad in her life: a father who'd left and never looked back, a mother who couldn't keep her promise not to die and a grandmother whose expectations she could never meet. When Trish had gotten on that plane after graduation, pregnant and alone, she'd been convinced her life was over before it had even begun.

Now she was starting to believe that her dreams could come true. One day perhaps the three of them might be a real family. Before that could happen, Jack and Tommy needed to know the truth. But when to tell them?

The question had been niggling at her for days. Part of her hesitation came from knowing they'd be angry she'd deceived them.

Trish exhaled a ragged breath. She could deal with the anger, but what if they refused to forgive her? If she lost them both...

Despair threatened to overwhelm her, but Trish shoved the worry aside. There was nothing she could do about that now. When the right time came, the only thing she could do was to be honest and hope they understood.

For now, she would just focus on enjoying everything that was right with her life. Trish took a long sip of the diet cola and swung slowly back and forth, listening as the faint buzz of the cicadas mingled with the chirp of crickets.

Her gaze lifted to the star-filled sky. Though Trish knew it was childish, she couldn't stop from making a wish on the first one that caught her eye.

"Got any chips to go with that soda?"

"Jack." Trish's head jerked up, her heart thumping noisily in her chest. From the looks of his suit and tie, he'd come straight from the chamber dinner to the steps of her porch. "What are you doing here?"

Jack's devastating smile took her breath away. "Someone told me this was the place to come for chips and soda."

"I'd have thought the rubber chicken would have filled you up," Trish said half-jokingly, knowing she would have given anything to eat that chicken.

"It ended up being prime rib and it was actually pretty good," Jack said. His gaze met hers. "But it wasn't any fun eating alone."

"But you didn't eat alone," Trish said. "There had to have been fifty people at that dinner."

"But you weren't there." His direct gaze met hers.

It was all Trish could do to keep a goofy smile from her face as warmth spread all the way to the tips of her painted toes.

But she smiled to herself as she got Jack his soda and a bag of chips.

She took a seat on the swing and Jack sat next to her. As they chatted companionably, a sense of déjà vu enveloped Trish. Talking about his evening reminded her of before, when she and Jack had led separate lives. When her only knowledge of his world had come from his stories. When she'd been the friend no one knew he had....

Trish shoved the silly thought aside. What had happened back then had nothing to do with their relationship now. *Nothing.*

Jack settled his arm around her shoulders, and Trish snuggled against him, inhaling the spicy scent of his cologne.

"How was KC?" Jack brushed his lips against her hair.

A shiver traveled down her spine. For a second she couldn't breathe, much less think what he was talking about.

"I didn't go," Trish said at last.

"You didn't?" Jack's voice reflected his surprise. "Why not?"

"When I got home, I was tired." Trish saw no need to mention that part of her exhaustion stemmed from fighting off Joe in accounting all week. The last thing she'd wanted to do was to spend the evening as Joe's 'date.' "I decided I'd rather stay home and hang out with my favorite guy."

Jack's brow furrowed in a frown, and a flash of jealousy crossed his face.

Though Trish was tempted to string him along, she didn't have the heart. "Did I mention my favorite guy is a fourth-grader? He's about five feet tall with dark-brown hair…"

"I get the picture." Jack's boisterous laugh was edged with relief.

"Tell me more about your evening," Trish said. "Did you have a good time?"

"It was just okay," Jack said. "But the emcee was terrific."

Trish rolled her eyes, and her laughter mingled with his. But when Jack took her hand and rubbed her palm gently with his thumb, the laughter died in her throat.

"Seriously." His gaze focused on her mouth. "I missed you tonight."

Then why didn't you ask me to go with you?

"You know, when I was out here earlier—" Trish shifted her gaze and stared into the darkness "—it reminded me of those nights I used to I sit on this very swing and wait for you."

"When I was walking up the drive, I thought of that, too," Jack admitted.

"We used to talk for hours." Trish exhaled a

deep sigh. "I thought I knew you better than I knew myself."

"You were doing better than I was." Jack gave a rueful laugh. "Back then I wasn't sure who I was or what I wanted."

"And now?" Trish's voice sounded strained even to her own ears. "Do you know what you want?"

In the dim glow of the porch light, Jack's expression softened. His hand rose to cup her cheek.

"I know exactly what I want," he said in a hushed whisper.

Trish's breath caught in her throat as his mouth covered hers. She wrapped her arms around his neck and returned his kiss.

He'd been a boy back then. Now he was a man. And he wanted *her*. She'd been wrong to doubt his love. Trish opened her mouth, and he deepened the kiss. The night stood still.

"Let's go inside." His breath was warm against her ear, and his words so soft she wondered if she'd only imagined them.

She arched her head and he nuzzled her neck.

"Don't you like it out here?" Her words came out as a moan.

His hands skimmed up her sides, stopping just below her breasts. "It would be more private inside."

It had been so long since she'd been close to Jack in that special way. An overwhelming desire surged through Trish, and she wanted nothing more than to take Jack's hand and lead him up those long narrow stairs to her bedroom.

Let's make love all night long.

The words ran through Trish's mind like the refrain to a song.

"Oh, Trish. It could be so good," Jack said, nibbling on her ear.

You're both adults, a tiny voice inside whispered. What's wrong with showing him how much you love him?

Trish's mind whirled and swirled, a muddled mass of confusing thoughts and emotions. It was hard to think with him so near. He was so close she could feel his warmth, smell his cologne and almost taste the sweetness of his kiss.

She moistened her lips with her tongue.

His eyes darkened.

He leaned forward and took her hands. "Let me love you."

Trish stared. His words were *close* to what she wanted to hear. But the question was, were they close enough?

"Is something wrong?" he said.

"No. Nothing is wrong," Trish lied.

How could she tell Jack that it wasn't so much what he'd said as what he hadn't said? What he'd *never* said to her. "It's just that it has been a long week and I am tired. I'd better call it a night."

"You want to go to bed? Alone?" At any other

time the confused look in his eyes would have been almost funny.

She met his gaze and her heart twisted. If only her answer could be different. But the one time she'd let her heart lead the way it had ended up broken.

Now she was older.

And wiser.

She couldn't make that same mistake again.

Chapter Twelve

Jack had barely shoved his bag of golf clubs into the back of his Jeep when his cell phone rang. He smiled.

Trish had already called him twice, and it wasn't even nine o'clock. Although he still had five minutes to go before he had to be at her house, he had no doubt it was her on the phone, calling to make sure he was on his way over.

He flipped open the phone. "I'm just leaving."

"Jack. It's Missy." Her words tumbled over each other. "Derek just called. He's in town and he says he's coming over."

His chest tightened at the fear in her voice. "Have you called the sheriff?"

"A lot of good it did me." The disgust in her voice didn't quite hide the fear. "He and Howie are working a bad accident over on the highway. Fred asked if Derek had threatened me and I told him no. At least not this time. He said he'd get here as soon as he can, but—"

"Missy?" Jack prompted when she didn't continue.

"Fred didn't seem to understand that Derek didn't threaten me before and look what happened." Missy's voice trembled. "I'm scared, Jack. Kaela and I are here alone."

"I'll be right over." Jack slid behind the wheel and turned on the ignition. The Jeep's engine roared to life.

"Are you sure?"

He could hear the relief in her voice. Jack thought of the golf outing. He knew Trish really wanted him to go. But there would be other events. This was an emergency. Surely she'd understand that he couldn't let a friend down.

Reveling in the icy coolness of the clubhouse, Trish wondered what she'd been thinking. What had ever made her believe that hitting a little ball around a course in hundred-degree heat would be fun?

"Where's the boyfriend?" Joe sidled up to her in the buffet line, his nonchalant demeanor at odds with the keen interest in his eyes.

"He couldn't make it." After three hours of hearing the same question, Trish's answer was automatic. Why had she ever mentioned that Jack would be coming with her?

"Some of us are starting to wonder if you've been making the guy up."

His tone was teasing, and Trish forced a smile, though she found the whole situation anything but amusing.

"Oh, he's very real." She was pleased her voice came out smooth and detached, as if Jack's not showing up was merely an inconvenience and nothing more. When he'd called this morning with some nonsensical babble about an emergency involving a friend, she'd responded in the same manner. Though she was disappointed, deep down she hadn't been that surprised.

"Trish. Over here."

Trish shifted her gaze across the room.

Ron Royer stood next to a table filled with people. He smiled and pulled out the last empty chair at his table, motioning her over.

Trish groaned to herself. The last thing she wanted to do now was to sit with Jack's old friend. But what was her choice? To sit with Joe?

Making her decision, Trish said goodbye to a clearly disappointed Joe and wove her way across the crowded dining area.

Ron made quick work of the introductions. Surprisingly, Jack's name didn't come up at all until Trish was halfway through her meal. And then Jane Royer, who up to this point had let her husband do most of the talking, brought him up. "Someone told me you were bringing Jack Krieger as your guest today. Did he decide not to come?"

"Jane." Ron shot his wife a disapproving look. "That's quite enough."

"Jack *had* planned to come." Trish wondered how many more times she was going to have to allude to some vague "emergency" before the day was done. "But then—"

"You don't need to explain," Ron said. "I told Jane last week that Jack and Missy were back together. Obviously, she didn't make the connection. I'm sorry she brought it up."

Trish's breath caught in her throat.

Jack and Missy? Together again? She shook her head. Impossible.

Jane stared at her husband. "You never told me Jack and Missy were dating."

"I most certainly did." Ron met his wife's gaze head-on. His easy smile did nothing to soften the sharpness of his tone. "It was the night I went to the chamber dinner in Lynnwood. I told you that Jack was there with Missy."

"You mentioned she was there. And that Jack was the emcee," Jane said. "But you didn't say anything about them dating."

"I said they came together, didn't I?" Ron said. "And I said they left together, didn't I?"

Trish clenched her hands into fists in her lap, her nails digging into her palms.

"Well, yes," Jane said reluctantly.

"How could I have made it any clearer? Tell me that."

Jane's lips tightened at her husband's terse tone, but she didn't answer.

An awkward silence descended over the table. Though Trish shouldn't have been surprised that she'd been betrayed again, she was. And if she expected it to hurt less the second time around, she was wrong.

Dead wrong.

"Jack!" His mother looked up from her dining room table, surprise blanketing her face. "I thought you and Trish would be in Kansas City by now."

"She's there." Jack pulled out a chair and took a seat. "But something came up and I had to cancel."

"I hope it was important," his mother said with a frown. "Trish had really been looking forward to you going with her."

"I know she was," Jack said with a sigh. "But this couldn't be helped."

Derek had been on his best behavior, but Jack didn't regret the choice he'd made. Missy had good reason to be afraid of her ex-husband. And though nothing had happened this time, who knew what Derek might have done if Missy had been alone?

Even though Derek's appearance had been brief, by the time Jack had left Missy's house, it had been too late to catch up with Trish. Feeling strangely unsettled, he'd headed over to his mother's house hoping he could persuade her to grab a cup of coffee with him.

"What are you doing?" Jack stared at the normally immaculate table, now littered with photo albums and half-opened cardboard boxes.

"Tommy is helping me organize my pictures. Here he is now." His mother shifted her gaze to the doorway, and Jack realized he'd forgotten his mother was watching Tommy. "Did you have any trouble finding them?"

"Nope." Tommy crossed the room and sat the box on the edge of the table, next to Jack's mother. "They were in the attic next to the sewing machine, just like you said."

The boy shot Jack a puzzled look. "Aren't you supposed to be at that golf thing with my mom?"

"Something came up," Jack said with a shrug.

"You have time to shoot some hoops?"

Jack gestured to the pile of pictures his mother had already dumped from the box Tommy had brought from the attic. "I would, but it looks like you two have a lot of work here."

"I'd rather play basketball with you," Tommy said.

"Didn't you promise to help my mother?" Jack said.

Tommy turned a pleading gaze to Connie Krieger, but she didn't seem to notice. Her entire attention was focused on the photo in her hand.

Her mother's lips tipped up in smile. "Jack was such a pretty baby."

Tommy leaned over to get a better look. "Let me see."

"Pretty?" Jack glanced at the photo and chuckled. "With all those rolls of fat how can you tell?"

"You weren't fat," his mother chided. "You were just a big boy. My goodness, what do you expect? You were almost ten pounds when you were born."

"I was nine and a half pounds." Tommy smiled at Jack.

Jack's brows furrowed in a frown. "But I thought you were premature?"

"What does that mean?" Tommy asked.

"Born earlier than expected," Mrs. Krieger explained.

"I wasn't that." Tommy shook his head vigorously. "I was late. My mom said they even had to give her medicine to make me come out."

"Are you sure?" Jack pinned the boy with his gaze.

Tommy hesitated, clearly confused by Jack's intense scrutiny. "That's what she said."

A viselike tightness gripped Jack's chest in a stranglehold.

"Jack, lay off the boy," his mother said, a hint

of warning in her tone. "Early? Late? What does it matter, anyway?"

Jack wanted to tell his mother that it mattered a lot. That if Tommy *was* born full-term it might mean that the boy was his son. *And* her grandson. But Jack remained silent. Tommy could be mistaken, and he wasn't going to say anything until he was sure of the facts.

"Look at this picture, Jack." His mother picked up another photo in a valiant attempt to change the subject. "You would have been about Tommy's age. I always loved it when you wore your Boy Scout uniform."

Jack took the photograph from her and dutifully glanced at it. He knew exactly when this picture was taken. The merit badge he was holding up had been a difficult one and he'd received it the day after his tenth birthday.

He stared idly at his boyish features. His hair had been cut short back then, much like Tommy's was now.

Jack's gaze shifted from the picture to Tommy, and he caught his breath. The boy in front of him looked so much like the picture of his ten-year-old self, he couldn't believe he hadn't seen it before. The resemblance was positively uncanny.

In that moment any doubts Jack had about the identity of Tommy's father vanished.

"Let me see." Tommy took the photo from

Jack's hand. "Wow. You sure did have a lot of badges."

"Yes, I did." Jack couldn't keep from staring at his son. He wondered how his mother had failed to see the resemblance.

"I was a Cub Scout once," Tommy said. "I liked it a lot. But I was never a Boy Scout."

"If you liked Scouting so much, why did you quit?" Jack asked.

The boy shifted uncomfortably under Jack's unwavering stare.

"I dunno." Tommy shrugged.

"You must have had a reason." Suddenly no detail of Tommy's past life was too small, too insignificant. Jack wanted to hear it all.

"I guess because they started doing a lot of things with dads," Tommy said. "And I didn't have one."

But you did have a dad, Jack wanted to scream. One who would have given anything to have gone on those camp-outs with you.

Regret mingled with his mounting anger. He'd missed so much. Years that could never be made up. Precious time lost for both him and Tommy. What reason could Trish have had to keep such a secret? None of it made any sense.

When Trish got back from Kansas City, she had some explaining to do. Until then, he'd keep his mouth shut.

Jack's gaze shifted to Tommy, wishing he could

tell him right now that he was his father and assure him that he would never have to worry about being without a dad ever again. Because Jack was in his life now and that's right where he intended to stay.

Nothing, and no one, was ever going to come between them again.

Chapter Thirteen

Trish had just unlocked her front door when Jack appeared out of nowhere and brushed past her, his long, determined strides headed straight for her living room.

Fuming at such audacity, she followed him, her hands clenched into fists at her sides. How dare he think he could just waltz into her home anytime he pleased?

"I don't appreciate your barging in like this." Trish stood in the doorway of her living room and folded her arms across her chest, feeling strangely vulnerable under his intense stare. "What's going on here? And where's Tommy?"

Jack leaned back against the sofa, but his pose was anything but relaxed. "Tommy is at his grandmother's house."

"Grandmother?" Trish's breath caught in her throat. "My mother is dead."

"Mine isn't." Though Jack's voice was soft and low, a chill traveled up Trish's spine.

"I'm afraid I don't understand."

"Yes, you do."

"Actually I don't have a clue." Trish forced a little laugh and nervously brushed back a strand of hair with one hand. "Of course your mother is like a grandmother to Tommy…"

"She's his grandmother because I'm Tommy's father." Jack's harsh tone was edged with steel. "You know, I never could figure out why you were in such a hurry to leave Lynnwood after graduation. Now I know. You were pregnant."

Trish's breath caught in her throat. Unlike before, when his tone had been questioning, this time he said it as a statement of fact.

She took a deep breath and smiled as if Jack's words were merely amusing and not the truth. Though she had planned to tell him, she didn't want it to be like this. "C'mon Jack. We've been through this before. Tommy's father and I met in D.C.—"

"Another lie." Jack's unflinching gaze met hers. "You also told me Tommy was premature."

"He *was* premature," she said. Trish could only hope the desperation racing through her body didn't show in her face. "Two months early."

"He weighed almost ten pounds, Trish," Jack

said flatly. "And Tommy told me they had to give you medicine because he was overdue."

"Is that what you were doing while I was gone?" Trish's voice rose. "Interrogating my son?"

Jack blew out a harsh breath. "For God's sake Trish, I know the truth. At least be honest now."

Resigned to the inevitable, she slowly nodded.

Disappointment warred with the anger on Jack's face. "Tell me one thing. After all we shared, how could you do it? How could you have my son and not even tell me?"

"After all we shared?" Trish shoved a momentary twinge of guilt aside and reminded herself she had no reason to feel guilty. "Give me a break. I didn't mean anything to you."

"How can you say that? We were friends, good friends. And—"

"I wasn't your friend," Trish spat out the word. "I was convenient. I was a lonely fat girl, who was stupid enough to spend my entire senior year in high school groveling for a few scraps of your attention. Of course I only saw you after you were through having fun with your real friends—the friends you weren't ashamed to be seen with."

Tears filled her eyes, but Trish angrily brushed them aside.

"I was never ashamed of you—" Jack's eyes flashed "—or our friendship."

"I'm not stupid, Jack." Trish stepped back, his

vehement denial taking her by surprise. "I heard you in the hallway, telling your friends—" she faltered, not having known she would say this "—telling them…that you'd never lower yourself to be with someone like me."

Jack paused as if searching his memory. She could almost see the moment he remembered. Compassion filled his gaze and he reached for her.

She jerked away, fighting the tears. "Maybe I wasn't the prettiest girl. But I was a good person. *I* was a good friend to you. And I didn't deserve to be used like that!"

"You've got it all wrong," Jack said. "I was only trying to protect you."

"What about Missy?" Trish said, her voice heavy with sarcasm. "Did I get that wrong, too?"

"What are you talking about?"

"Do you deny you took her to the chamber dinner?" Trish said.

"She needed a ride." He met her gaze, and his tone was level.

"Did she need a kiss, too?"

The muscle in his jaw twitched, and she knew her shot in the dark had hit its mark.

"Missy and I are just friends."

"And today?" Trish asked, surprised she could sound so calm when her heart was breaking. "Are you going to deny you were with her?"

"Let me explain—"

"Don't bother." Trish moved to the door and jerked it open. "Get out and don't come back."

Jack remained seated. "Trish, you need to listen to me."

"I don't need to do anything."

"Fine." Heaving an exasperated sigh, Jack stood. He crossed the room and brushed past Trish. In the doorway he stopped and turned. "When you calm down, we'll talk."

"Stay out of my life, Jack." Trish started to close the door. "And out of my son's."

Jack stopped the door's movement with his foot. "Let me make one thing clear. You may have kept Tommy from me up to now, but no more. Like it or not, I will be a part of his life." He stepped onto the porch. "I *am* going to call you later and we *will* talk."

Trish slammed the door shut. Leaning against the heavy oak, she slid to the floor, burying her face in her hands.

All these months she'd convinced herself Jack had changed. But he hadn't. He was arrogant and self-centered. And now he knew Tommy was his son.

Hot tears streamed down her cheeks. Why had she ever left Washington? She'd had friends there. People who cared. And if she'd held out a few months longer, she would even have had a terrific job.

Trish took a quick, sharp breath and scrambled

to her feet. She headed for the desk, impatiently wiping away the tears.

Riffling through the top drawer, Trish finally found the long narrow envelope. A business card still tucked inside held the name and number of the human-resource manager. Though she didn't expect to reach anyone on a Saturday night, she picked up the phone, dialed the number and left a message. Satisfied she'd done all she could for now, Trish placed the phone back on its cradle and sat back in the chair.

By the end of the month she and Tommy would be back in D.C. and Jack Krieger would be nothing more than a bad memory.

First thing Monday morning Trish got a call confirming that the position was hers. She made plans to move back to Washington immediately. Though the job wouldn't start for a few months, what little savings she'd managed to amass since moving to Lynnwood would tide her over until the new job started.

When she got home she deleted all the messages on her answering machine. Yesterday Jack had called twice. She'd let the machine pick up both times. He obviously thought they still needed to talk. Trish knew better. What else was there to say?

If only she could just pick up and leave right now instead of waiting until the end of the week. But she consoled herself with the knowledge that once she left, she'd never have to see Jack Krieger or this town ever again.

Tommy sure wasn't going to be happy about it. He'd grown to love Lynnwood. When she'd picked him up at Julie's house, all he could talk about was some basketball camp he and Matt planned to attend. She hadn't the heart to tell him he'd be long gone before that camp even started.

"I'm going to shoot some hoops before dinner." Tommy stood on the landing to the stairs, a basketball spinning between his fingers.

Trish hesitated. Would now be a good time to talk to him?

He took the remaining steps two at a time and headed for the door.

"Hold on." Trish wiped her suddenly sweaty hands against her skirt. "I need to talk to you."

With an audible groan, Tommy turned. "I already said I was sorry, didn't I?"

Puzzled, Trish paused until she remembered that she'd chided him about leaving the air conditioner running full blast while they were gone. "It's not about the air conditioner."

"Then what?" He impatiently glanced at the door.

"I have some exciting news." Trish took a deep breath. "I've decided to accept the job with that firm in D.C."

Tommy's brow furrowed and in that moment he

looked so much like his father that Trish's heart twisted.

"They'll let you work from here?"

"No." Trish forced a smile. "That's the exciting part. You and I are moving back to Washington."

Tommy's hands tightened around the basketball. "I like it here."

"I know you do," she said in a soothing voice. "But you liked it there, too. Remember?"

"Matt and I have plans. We have basketball camp, and we're going to be on the same football team." His jaw jutted out. "I don't want to move."

"I'm afraid you don't have a choice." Trish kept her tone level. "You and I are a package deal. Where I go you go. So, I need you to start getting your things together. We'll be flying back day after tomorrow."

"But you like it here, too." Panic edged Tommy's voice. "You said so."

"I did," Trish said. "But things have changed."

"Well, I still like it here. And I'm not moving." The basketball dropped to the carpeted floor with a thud. Tommy lifted his chin. "You can't make me."

"I'm your mother." She met his defiant gaze with an unflinching one of her own. "You'll do as I say."

"I'm not leaving!" Tommy whirled and headed up the stairs. In a few minutes the sound of his bedroom door slamming reverberated throughout the house.

Trish squared her shoulders, gritted her teeth and headed up the stairs. But by the time she got to the top, she'd cooled off. She paused outside his door and wondered if it might not be best to give Tommy some space. With a resigned sigh Trish returned to the living room.

Tommy ignored her call to dinner, even when she told him she'd made his favorite, spaghetti and meatballs. Though she wasn't particularly hungry, Trish made an effort to eat. But the pasta tasted like wallpaper paste, and she dumped it into the garbage after a couple of bites. She tried to read but her mind wandered, replaying that last conversation with Jack over and over in her mind.

Trish glanced at the phone. Should she call Jack? Give him a chance to explain?

And then what? Despite strong, solid evidence to the contrary, you'll believe him?

The thought was so close to the truth that Trish flushed guiltily. Was she the world's biggest fool? Hadn't she learned her lesson about Jack Krieger? Hadn't she learned that despite that incredible smile and honest face, she couldn't believe a word he said?

With a resigned sigh, Trish flipped off the evening news and headed to her bedroom. On the way she stopped at Tommy's door. She and Tommy had never gone to bed angry, and she wasn't about to start a new tradition.

"Tommy." Trish rapped lightly on his door. "Can I come in?"

When she didn't get a response, she tapped the door again. "Honey? I just want to say good-night."

This time she didn't wait for an answer. The doorknob turned easily in her hand and she pushed it open. She moved quietly to her son's bedside.

Trish reached down, but instead of her son's shoulder, she encountered only softness. She pulled back the quilt and stared. The lumpy shape was a row of artfully placed pillows. Her son had deliberately tried to make her think he was in bed asleep.

Her gaze darted around the empty room, stopping on a piece of white notebook paper propped against the dresser mirror. With a feeling of dread, Trish moved quickly across the room and grabbed the sheet. Opening it, she immediately recognized Tommy's childish scrawl.

Mom,
I'm sorry but I'm not leaving. Don't worry. I can take care of myself.
    Love,

                            Tommy

A vise-like tightness gripped Trish's chest until she could barely breathe. She read the note again, then crumpled it in her hand. Where could he have gone? She glanced out the lace curtains into the darkness, noticing for the first time that the screen had been pushed out.

Her heart pounded in her chest, and panic filled every pore. Her little boy was out there in the night all alone.

Dear God, what was she going to do now?

Chapter Fourteen

Trish raced down the stairs and headed outside. She quickly checked the garage before slipping through the hedge and heading next door. Connie Krieger's house was dark, but Trish rang the bell and banged on the door, anyway.

When no one answered she ran back home and called the police. The dispatcher answered on the first ring. "Sheriff's office, state your emergency."

"I need to report a missing child." Trish's voice broke, and she stifled a sob. Dear God, what was she going to do if they didn't find him?

By the time she'd checked with the other neighbors, Fred had arrived with his deputy in tow. His last question before leaving was pointed and direct: Could Tommy's father possibly be involved? Startled, Trish said no without thinking. But after the sheriff left, she began to wonder if maybe Tommy could have gone to Jack's house.

She called Jack, but got a busy signal. Stifling a curse, Trish dropped her cellular phone into her jacket pocket and grabbed her car keys. In five minutes she was on his porch, thankful that his lights were on. At least he was home.

The bell hadn't even finished ringing when the door swung open.

Delight quickly replaced the surprise on his face. "Trish, I'm glad you came over."

Hope rose inside her. "So he's here?"

His brows drew together. "Who?"

"Tommy." She craned her neck, trying to see around him.

"What makes you think he's with me?"

"C'mon, Jack." Trish's voice trembled. "Just tell me. Is he here or not?"

Concern filled Jack's gaze. "I haven't seen Tommy since Saturday."

Her heart plummeted. Though she hadn't really believed Tommy would be here, she'd still hoped. Trish took a deep breath, wondering where she should look next. The sheriff said he'd call with any news, but that didn't mean she couldn't search for her son while she waited. As long as she had her phone, he could reach her.

Trish pulled the cell phone from her pocket and made sure it was still on. "Thanks, anyway."

She turned to go, but Jack grabbed her arm. "Not so fast. What's going on? Where's Tommy?"

"I don't know." Her shoulders suddenly slumped and tears filled her eyes. "He...he ran away."

"Ran away?" Jack's face paled. "Are you sure?"

She nodded. "He left a note."

"But why?"

"He was upset." Trish couldn't quite meet Jack's gaze. Though she knew she'd done nothing wrong, guilt sluiced through her. "But I never thought he'd do anything like this."

"Have you called the sheriff?"

Trish nodded. "And I've checked with all the neighbors as well as Tommy's friends. But...nothing."

She raised her gaze and her lips trembled. "I can't tell you how much I hoped he'd be here."

"So you told him I was his father," Jack said. "And he didn't take it well."

"That wasn't it at all," she said. "He still doesn't know about you."

"Then why was he upset?"

She hesitated. "I told him we were moving back to D.C."

Jack's eyes widened, and he had the look of someone who'd just been punched in the stomach.

"You can't be serious. You want to take my son and move halfway across—" Jack stopped himself midsentence. He paused and drew a ragged breath. "That's not important now. We need to find Tommy."

Trish didn't protest when Jack wrapped a reassuring arm around her shoulder and led her down the hall to the kitchen. Sitting across from her at the table, he listened intently while she outlined the events of the evening. "My first thought was he'd be at your mother's house, but she wasn't home."

"She's visiting her sister in Topeka for a few days. I'm surprised she didn't tell you she was going to be gone."

"She might have tried," Trish said, thinking of the phone calls she hadn't answered.

"It doesn't matter," Jack said. "The only thing that matters is finding our son."

Trish nodded. Jack was right. Nothing mattered except Tommy. "We'll find him, won't we?"

"Of course we will," Jack said with a bold confidence Trish found reassuring. "He'll be in his own bed before midnight."

But midnight came and went. As the sun rose, worry replaced the confidence in Jack's gaze. Every lead had gone nowhere. She returned to her own house as the sheriff had suggested "in case the boy decides to come home," but Jack headed out to look some more. He said he'd go crazy if he just sat around waiting.

At eight o'clock the back screen door creaked

open, and Trish turned. Her flicker of hope died when she saw Missy's face peering in.

"Can I come in?"

"Sure. But if you're looking for Jack, he just left."

Confusion filled Missy's gaze. "Why would I be looking for him? It's you and Tommy I'm concerned about."

"I'll get you some coffee." Trish rose and poured a cup of coffee and set it on the table. She couldn't be rude. It certainly wasn't Missy's fault that Jack liked her best. And Missy *had* been one of the volunteers who'd spent the night combing the nearby countryside searching for Tommy.

Missy took a seat at the table opposite Trish and added a spoonful of sugar to her coffee. "Have you heard anything?"

Trish's heart tightened. "Not a word."

"He'll be fine." Missy smiled reassuringly. "Lynnwood is a safe town."

"I know, but he's just a little boy." Trish swallowed past the lump in her throat. "And I love him so much."

"I know you do," Missy said softly.

"I'm sorry." Tears welled in Trish's eyes and she wiped at them with a paper napkin. "I don't mean to sit here blubbering."

"Hey, I'm a mother, too. I understand completely." Missy patted Trish's hand. "We'd do anything to protect our children. That's why I freaked when Derek showed up unexpectedly on Saturday.''

Trish just nodded. She had no clue what Missy was talking about and she was too tired to ask.

"It wasn't just me I was worried about," Missy said. "It was Kaela. When Derek is in one of his moods, he's capable of just about anything. With my dad out of town, I didn't know what to do. Thank God I got hold of Jack. I hope he told you how sorry I was for messing up your plans."

"The golf outing." Suddenly it all made sense.

"He really wanted to go, but he said you'd understand. I don't know if I would have been so understanding." Missy smiled. "But I guess that's why he loves you and not me."

"Loves me?" Trish stared. "Where'd you get that idea?"

"Jack told me."

"When?"

Missy stared curiously at Trish. "He told me he was in love with you the day of the chamber dinner. That was the day he gave me a ride because my car was in the shop. Afterward, he took me home."

"Was that before or after the kiss?" Trish lifted a questioning brow.

"He told you about that?" Missy reddened and squirmed in her seat. "Jack's a good guy and it's no secret that I've always liked him. But the kiss was my idea, not his. And I won't be doing that again. He made it clear he wasn't interested."

He tried to tell me the truth. But I was too pig-headed to listen. Trish's heart clenched and she buried her face in her hands. How could she have been so foolish?

Missy rose and circled the table, patting Trish's shoulder. "It'll be okay—"

As if on cue, the screen door banged open.

"Look who I found," Jack said in an exuberant tone.

"Tommy." Trish shot from her chair, her heart in her throat. She enveloped her son in a massive bear hug. "Oh, Tommy. I was so scared."

"I'm sorry, Mom." Tears glistened in the boy's eyes. "I didn't mean to worry you."

"I need to be running along." Missy grabbed her purse and headed for the door.

"Missy." Trish turned, but her arm remained firmly around Tommy. "Thank you so much...for everything."

"No problem," Missy said with an understanding smile. "After all, what are friends for?"

"Maybe we can get together for lunch soon?" Trish said.

Missy smiled. "I'd like that."

Trish pulled Tommy close for another hug, her words muffled against his hair. "I love you so much. Don't ever run from me again. Together we can work anything out. Understand?"

Tommy's boyish arms tightened around her. "I love you, too, Mom."

She kissed the top of his head and brushed away a tear.

"And now, my boy—" Trish smiled "—I think we need to run you a hot bath and get some food in you. What do you think?"

Tommy nodded, then his gaze shifted to his feet. "Are we still going to move?"

"We'll talk about that later," Trish said.

"But—"

"Tommy," Jack said firmly, sounding to Trish's ears very much like a father. "Your mother said later."

Jack gave Tommy a smile as the boy headed up the stairs, then turned to Trish. "I called the sheriff and told him the good news. He'll be calling in the volunteers."

Trish gestured to the chair. "Can you stay for a while? I want to hear every detail."

"I don't know why I didn't think of it sooner." Jack pulled a chair out from the table and took a seat, fatigue edging his eyes. "A couple of weeks ago I'd shown Tommy and Matt an old tree house some friends and I had built in that grove of trees down by the Larkins' pond. The boys were fascinated by it. When I got there this morning, I found Tommy fast asleep."

"I don't know how I can ever thank you," Trish said.

"Don't move back to D.C.," Jack said.

Trish's gaze dropped for a moment to her coffee

cup, and she chose her words carefully. "I'm surprised you still want me to stay. After the way I acted."

"I should have told you that Missy was at the dinner." Jack's voice was husky. "And that she was the reason I couldn't go—"

"I was stubborn and headstrong. When you offered to explain, I refused to listen." Trish met his gaze. "I did the same thing when I was eighteen."

"Trish, about the prom…"

"Jack." Trish raised her hand, shaking her head. She'd made her share of mistakes, too. "You don't have to explain."

"I don't want there to be any more secrets or misunderstandings between us," Jack said.

Trish met his gaze. "I don't want there to be, either."

"Just promise you'll hear me out before you interrupt. Okay?"

Trish wasn't sure she wanted to hear what he had to say, but she owed it to him to listen now. She nodded.

"Ron and Chip put us in that closet hoping we'd have sex."

"So it was all planned." Trish couldn't stem the rush of disappointment that coursed through her body.

"You said you'd hear me out." Jack reminded her. "Keep in mind they lured me there just as they did you."

"But why me?"

"You were available."

"Of course I was. Even my blind date didn't want to be seen with Fatty Patty." Trish's heart twisted.

"Don't say that." Jack leaned forward, his eyes blazing. "You looked beautiful. You *were* beautiful. That guy was a fool."

"If you thought I was so beautiful, why did you say what you did in that hallway?"

"I was trying to protect you," Jack said. "If I'd given them any indication that something had happened in that closet, Chip and Ron would have trashed your reputation."

"So you weren't ashamed of me?" Trish asked softly, hardly daring to hope.

Jack met her gaze. "I realized that night how important you were to me."

"But you didn't want anything to do with me after that. You never came around."

"Because you told me you were too busy to see me on Friday and Saturday nights," he said. "I could tell you were upset, so I thought I'd give you some space. The next thing I knew you were gone."

Trish realized with a pang of regret that he was right. She'd been so angry and hurt ten years ago, she'd avoided him completely.

"Well, I guess it's all water under the bridge,

anyway,'' Trish said with a heavy sigh. ''At least now we're clear on everything.''

''Not everything.'' Jack leaned forward across the table, and she could see the hurt in his eyes. ''Why didn't you tell me you were pregnant?''

''Because of what I overheard.''

Jack shook his head. ''There had to be more to it than that. You knew me. You had to know I would have been there for you.''

''I didn't know any such thing,'' Trish said. ''And even if you had stood by me, why would I have wanted someone in my life who seemed to be ashamed of me?''

Jack started to argue, then stopped and thought for a moment. He expelled a heavy sigh. ''You're right. I gave you no reason to trust me. Just like this Missy thing…''

''You don't need to explain,'' Trish said. ''She told me everything.''

''She did?''

''And I believe her,'' Trish said. ''Except the part about you loving me.''

''It's true,'' Jack said. ''I do love you.''

''You do?'' Trish's gaze widened and her heart picked up speed. ''But why didn't you tell me?''

''I was waiting for the right time,'' he said softly. ''And I'm thinking it might be now.''

Jack circled the table and pulled Trish to her feet. ''I realized tonight how precious life is, how precious you and Tommy are to me. I can't undo the past but I want to make it up to you. And to Tommy. I want the three of us to be a family. Will you marry me, Trish?''

"If you're worried about me taking Tommy away from you, don't be.'' Trish's heart raced but her words were careful and measured. "You're his father and he needs you. I realize that now. I'm not moving back to D.C., so if that's why you asked—''

"The reason I want to marry you is that I love you.'' Jack gazed softly into her eyes.

Trish's breath caught in her throat at finally hearing those long-awaited words. Could it be true?

"Trish?''

She searched his gaze. The look in his eyes was filled with such love and caring that she wondered how she'd missed seeing it before. Trish lifted a hand to his cheek. "I love you, too.''

"Then you'll marry me?''

Pure happiness welled up inside Trish. She couldn't keep the silly grin from her face. "Of course I'll marry you.''

At her words, a matching grin blanketed Jack's face. "I'll make you happy. I promise.''

He lowered his mouth to hers…

The sound of footsteps sounded on the hardwood floor.

Trish and Jack turned as one, lifting their gazes upward.

"Is it true?'' Tommy stood on the stairway, his

blue eyes large in his pale face. "Are you really my dad?"

An icy prickle slid down Trish's spine and the muscles of Jack's forearm hardened beneath her hand.

Jack nodded slowly. "Is that okay?"

Tommy stared for a moment, then shrugged. "Does this mean we don't have to move?"

Trish slanted a sideways glance at Jack before answering. "Only down the block. How does that sound?"

Tommy's tight expression relaxed into a smile and Trish released the breath she hadn't realized she'd been holding.

"Can I tell Matt?" Tommy said.

"Of course you can tell him," Jack said. "Tell anyone you want."

"Cool." Tommy scampered up the stairs without so much as a backward glance.

"He seems okay with it." Though this wasn't the way she would have chosen to tell Tommy, she'd dreaded the moment for so long it was a relief to have it over. "I think it's a good sign that he wants to tell people."

"I know how he feels," Jack said, kissing her softly on the lips. "I can't wait to tell everyone. If I could, I'd shout it from the rooftop."

Trish giggled at the thought of Jack on her steep roof. She sobered at the thought of him slipping....

"No roof for you. That would be way too dangerous.'' She fingered a button on his shirt. ''I wouldn't want anything to happen to my future husband.''

His gaze darkened and his hand captured hers. He brought it to his lips. ''Promise you'll marry me soon.''

She smiled in answer, and as his lips lowered to hers and his body pressed hard against her, Trish decided a quick wedding might be just the thing. After all, she'd waited a long time for her own Prince Charming. Now that she was back in his arms, she wasn't going to waste another precious minute apart.

Epilogue

Flowers filled every nook of the reception hall, and the sound of music mingled with laughter and conversation.

"I can't tell you how much I appreciate your helping me get this wedding arranged on such short notice." Trish smiled at her new mother-in-law.

Only two weeks had passed since Jack had proposed, and now they were husband and wife. She stared down at her ring, scarcely able to believe her dreams had come true. "It was like a miracle. Everything fell into place."

"It was fun." Connie Krieger brushed a piece of lint from Trish's wedding dress. Although Trish would have been happy being married in a nice dress with just family in attendance, Connie had insisted she deserved a "proper" wedding. "I'm glad you let me be a part of it."

Thanks to Connie, the "proper" wedding had also been one straight out of a fairy tale: from the church and reception hall flowing with spring flowers, to Trish's satin and lace wedding dress, to the three-tiered work of art the local baker called a cake.

They'd said their vows in front of a church filled with friends and family, surrounded by love. After the traditional kiss, they'd both hugged their son.

Trish smiled, thinking back to how well Tommy had adjusted to the news that Jack was his father. When he'd called Jack "Dad" for the first time at the prenuptial dinner, it had been the best wedding gift she could have received.

"A penny for your thoughts." Jack's arm slipped around her waist.

"I was just thinking how happy I am." She lifted her face to his. "That I've got everything I've ever wanted right here in this room."

"I can think of one more thing."

"What is that?"

"Mrs. Krieger, may I have this dance?" Jack grasped her waist and took her hand in a warm clasp.

The band began to play, and suddenly Trish and

Jack were out on the shiny wooden floor moving in time to the music.

"Do you realize we've never danced together before this?" Trish whispered, unprepared for the intimacy of the moment. "At least not to real music."

"There are a lot of other things we've never done together," Jack said softly against her ear. "Lots of things I'd like to do."

"You forget. We've already made love." Trish cleared her throat, embarrassed at the breathless quality of her voice. "Remember?"

She felt his hand on the bare skin exposed by the deep vee of the back of her dress. He slowly moved his hand up and down, the sensual movement taking her breath away.

"Of course I remember." Jack's smile widened, and his hand moved up her back to play with her hair. "But there's only so much one can do in a closet."

"And outside of a closet?" Trish glanced at him from underneath her eyelashes, a shiver of anticipation traveling up her spine.

"You'll find out tonight," Jack said. He brushed Trish's hair back from her face.

Her heart lurched at the gesture.

"Keep in mind," he said, cupping her chin tenderly in his warm hand. "We have forever."

Jack's lips closed over hers, and Trish had the distinct feeling that "forever" in this man's arms wouldn't be nearly long enough.

*   *   *   *   *

If you enjoyed
TRISH'S NOT-SO-LITTLE SECRET,
you'll love Cynthia Rutledge's next story for
Steeple Hill Love Inspired:

WEDDING BELL BLUES

Available in July 2002
Don't miss it!

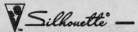

Silhouette Romance introduces tales of
enchanted love and things beyond explanation
in the new series

Soulmates

Couples destined for each other are brought
together by the powerful magic of love....

A precious gift brings
A HUSBAND IN HER EYES
by Karen Rose Smith (on sale March 2002)

Dreams come true in
CASSIE'S COWBOY
by Diane Pershing (on sale April 2002)

A legacy of love arrives
BECAUSE OF THE RING
by Stella Bagwell (on sale May 2002)

*Available at
your favorite retail outlet.*

Where love comes alive™